"Jarman works the nerve of friction between a person and the unbearable aspects of that person's life — not until something is solved, because a life is not something that can be solved, but rather until a trope, or a magical idea, begins to resonate. . . . These stories are so distilled and tightly focused that description and interaction with other characters have been boiled away, revealing a visceral, naked core of existence. . . . *19 Knives* is a sinuous, heart-breaking book that probes the fragility of human identity in a fresh, elemental way."

— *GLOBE AND MAIL*

"Mark Anthony Jarman's *[19 Knives]* is over far too soon. . . . But it resonates like a heat wave. . . Jarman has a gift for metaphor . . his view is so fresh it glows, and what he leaves behind in his darkly comic twilight is a glittering pile of broken rules. . . . I want more, but I'm happy to go back and read *19 Knives* again."

— *VANCOUVER SUN*

"Jarman's ingenuity is undeniable; his lingual dexterity is prodigious, at times downright acrobatic. . . . There are pieces in this collection that transcend the page, that force their way into the mind and take up residence like a determined squatter, refusing all attempt of eviction.... The stories are engaging ... enchanting, pulling the reader into worlds at once commonplace and hypnotic."

— *TORONTO STAR*

"Each of *19 Knives'* 14 stories integrates sparkling linguistic kinetics and honey-like narrative stickiness. Rejecting postmodern cynicism, Jarman celebrates life's ecstatic mysteries. Religious in their own way — finding meaning in music and everyday life, not empty theology — these stories shake like Muddy Waters riding a riff into the dark recesses of the night. Jarman gives us the best stuff. Solid gold."

—*QUILL & QUIRE* Starred Review

"The frenzied pace of Mark Anthony Jarman's *19 Knives* betrays the influence of the beat writers. But the dark figures who populate his devastating stories are more suggestive of David Foster Wallace.... Like a quart of hand-picked berries, the stories offer sweet stabs of delight with enough grit and pesticide to set your teeth on edge.'

— *ELM STREET*

"'Burn Man on a Texas Porch' [in *19 Knives*] . . . is not only the best [story] I've read in a year, it's probably one of the best ever written by a Canadian. It's focused, intense, colloquial and darkly funny — carefully crafted while remaining bracingly idiosyncratic.... You've got to love a writer in his late 40s who'll title a story after the cult band Guided by Voices, or who's as likely to quote Elliott Smith as Bertrand Russell."

— *EYE MAGAZINE*

"Jarman writes the way we'd like to talk, vocabulary tripping easily to tongue, snappy comebacks at just the right moment, never too formal or too painfully colloquial. He never makes a misstep, never puts words that are too big or too small in anyone's mouth; his dialogue sounds like it was transcribed from tape rather than imagined. The verisimilitude of his writing would be unbelievable were it not here on the page waiting to be read — and read it you should, for *19 Knives* is short fiction at its finest."

— *GEORGIA STRAIGHT*

"[*19 Knives*] made me feel as if I'd tripped and was stumbling off-balance into Jarman's words. Each sentence and paragraph runs headlong into the next one, and his adept use of metaphor helps fuel the momentum.... To say Jarman takes a few risks in his writing is like saying Evel Knievel sometimes bends the rules of the road."

— *NEW BRUNSWICK READER*

"*19 Knives* . . . packs a wallop. But it's not the kind of bone jarring crunch one has come to expect from much Canadian fiction.... No, this book is more like a well administered hip check, an open-ice hit that takes skill and finesse. . . . *19 Knives* is a book you'll want to return to again and again."

— *DAILY GLEANER* (Fredericton)

"Like Thornton Wilder, Jarman writes of the tiny, daily details without ever humiliating his everyman characters. His stories are sharp in memory, and their cut is clean and vivid, even as his narrators struggle for the exact, multi-affecting word."

— *MONDAY MAGAZINE (Victoria)*

–19–
Knives

ALSO BY MARK ANTHONY JARMAN

Dancing Nightly in the Tavern (stories)

Killing the Swan (poems)

New Orleans Is Sinking (stories)

Ounce of Cure (editor)

Salvage King, Ya! (novel)

Ireland's Eye (nonfiction)

My White Planet (stories)

–19– Knives

stories

Mark Anthony Jarman

Contents

Guided by Voices

For David Gedge

Fall from the Greyhound and my town seems so tiny: Smaller the cage, meaner the rat, allows my best friend John Stark Lee. All the stores have false wooden fronts pushed into each other on just one side of the street, a sandy road glowing under the walls and along the riverbank, and my bus idling under the single row of goldrush buildings with their gingerbread decks and narrow doors and sash windows and minarets facing the violent river like a frail resolute audience.

Hidden hilly lands stretch away east and west toward elegant storms, drums rolling, drums moving through your sternum or kidney. Our smoking skies perform and every spring the river jumps its pointless banks. Then later the river crawls back black and penitent over the sandy road. Got it out of its system.

September, spiderwebs everywhere and wild geese veering and a hawk low by the road. The juicy blackberries turn to hunks of fuzz, and stars like great gears roll over a blue norther.

The Red Planet Theatre has lately been converted to apartments, wallflower tenants creating novel curtains, making a home. No more movies Saturday night, no more *Eraserhead* on a double bill with *My Darling Clementine,* no more necking up high and throwing down our buttery garbage.

The post office is slick brick and does not fit our little town. The river once so stiff with fish you could walk across. The fish and game people are not sure what went wrong. They're taking samples, running tests. A young starcrossed couple from my old school drove right in the river and drowned last Valentine's. The strange thing is they hit the deep water in reverse, roaring backwards to the bottom. We can't leave it alone. Across the river you can see the new pastel prison and its floodlights the colour of television.

Across the river snowy lunar volcanoes and you see scars where American scientists with toothbrushes are digging up eggs and dinosaur bones, the bones of vegetarians and small fast mean meat-eaters who ran from here to Argentina when they were alive.

"Check these out!" says John Stark Lee, a pale-eyed magician pulling hickory drumsticks from his sleeves: his usual five finger discount. Scarred face where he ran his snowboard full bore into a copse of pointy trees, a grey branch breaking through his check two inches below his eye, John Lee eating and spitting wood and blood and one tooth into the snow on the steep mountain.

I just paid twenty-five dollars for a new blues harp in the music store, an instrument the size of two fingers, walked the dark boards to the elderly man at the cash register and I wanted to be Sonny Boy Williamson or Little Walter. Why do I feel like the stupid one for paying, feel like the sucker? John Lee's stolen drumsticks have those white plastic tips. I hate these rubber-legged noisy drummers.

"You're eighteen," I say. "You get busted you get a record now. You get a record then how you going to get a job?"

"Shut up, man, you're totally paranoid. I'm going to be a sixty-year-old punk rock grocery bagger," he says. "All right? Nice earring," he says. "I guess that's what the cool urbanite poseur dudes wear now."

"That's what we're wearing this year."

"Why you back here so often? Bella never wants to come back. She broke it off with me. You've been back about three times already. You flunking out?"

"I'm doing all right."

"Yeah, I bet you fit in fine. You homesick or something?"

"As if."

"Bella's gone weird on me. Piss me off something fierce. I'm not supposed to call her anymore. Sicks the law on me. You see her? You see her around, huh? Maybe you *study?*"

"I see her once in a while."

"Yeah I bet you see her some."

Where Marshall-Wells once was I lean against an old wooden fence, trying to look relaxed, trying to look happy, wanting to be happy, my nose full of the smell of mowed bunchgrass and bungalows and lilac trees. Somewhere close an engine's even cadence, men working over their insults under the evening map of branches. Tonight they are going to corner the boys from Alberta, make them pay for being from Alberta. The fights won't start for a few hours; this is a peaceful time. I love a good engine, hearing it turn over without hesitation.

The metal paint in the sky where tiny yellow birds zip by our heads and the ancient pine fence gives way right where I'm leaning, a scaly section falling over, almost taking me with it. Then the weight of its slow cracking drags down another thirty feet of knotholes. I seem to be attacking the avenues and entropy of my old lopsided town; I'm chewing the scenery, as they say in Hollywood. An engine revs and an elderly woman's words call down the busted fence and darkening road, "Boys, you better pick that mess up this instant!!"

John Stark Lee laughs, loves this noisy destruction. John Stark Lee gets some velocity, jumping and yelling and laughing at me: "Way to go Adam! Are we smart or what! You're a clown!"

"You heard me, young man!" Her words fainter as we flee. This reminds me of junior high: the centre of attention and not wanting to be. This reminds me of all the way back to kindergarten, maybe birth.

I have probably been within several feet of John Stark Lee's stern grey eyes every day from kindergarten. At least until last year. John Stark Lee is sharp, a fever spider inside, but he's never done well in school; more into new bands and boosting and snowboarding. Had radar for good new bands; liked Guided by Voices or the Giggling Faggots or the Picassoles way before anyone had heard of them. And he's a possessed nutter on a snowboard, knees bent, arms out, living in light over the ozone clouds. One step ahead of all of us on the plank and one step behind in school. Did not profit at school. Flunking school. His father who was a nice guy but looked like Hitler drove us right to the school's door and John Stark Lee still skipped class: stride in and stride right out the other side. Not in the cards.

"In this family we never had a quitter," his parents tell him.

"You know you're killing your mother," his father says.

"You know you're killing your father," his mother says.

Inside Sneaky Pete's we order at the front and pay in advance. John Stark Lee pays his tab with a mixed heap of coins. I pay mine with a twenty. They're playing the *White Album:* "Back in the USSR," "Glass Onion," number 9, number 9.

John Stark Lee picks a corner table and we wait for our numbers to come up. We don't talk but we're used to that. At school people get uncomfortable with silence, think silence a bad sign, and they talk just to hear themselves, to hear voices wrap like wool scarves around their heads.

What I could say: You ever going to finish school?

What he could reply: Fat chance, I'll never go back to school.

What John Stark Lee does say: "Oh, my darling mother drove into a Charolais milk cow by the railroad bridge, cow's big head came right through the window and dislocated her shoulder. Too surprised to give it a whack on the nose. My mother had to go to the hospital but the cow walked away. She made the paper. Her, not the milk cow, well both. Day and night you can find my old man playing Texas Hold 'Em Poker at the casino and he won't even take down the goddam Christmas lights. Mookie and the old Lowell gang, they're into carpeting, ornamental shrubs. New jobs, new girlfriends, new houses, or they've moved, hate me, whatever. . . . Same old same old. No one lately has said, John Lee I could fall for you in a big way. I am withering bigtime, bud, I'm becoming serious hind tit here, a small town joke. No more Navy rum. Woke up on the drunk tank floor and this space cadet from Kamloops with no shirt standing over me saying, 'Yeah I was at my sister's place and I beat the snot out of all her neighbours for looking at me weird.' He wanted to buy my shirt off me. Do you know what those drunk tank floors are like? Hell yes you can buy my shirt. This was when I wanted that 4 x 4, was saving up and working, working, working the assembly line — non-stop headless chickens coming at me, even in my dreams, dreaming headless fucking chickens and HEY, no more Navy rum for this cowboy"

"Pretty fucked up, bud. Our numbers are up."

He loads up with black pepper and apple salsa and jalapenos, loads his plate.

"Good food, good meat, yay Lord, let's eat."

"Down the hatch, bud."

I notice a woman, a bit older than us, staring at me. The woman mumbles something to herself, then stands and walks toward me. She's wearing fur boots and a ski jacket, though it's not cold in here or even down by the windy river. Her striped pants shift and undulate; the stripes seem alive and her outfit matches no era I can recall, a netherworld style that seems outside of recognized decades or fashion, like Astroturf or astronauts or eleventh-hour accordions. She has incubated, rebuilt memory. I see her but I'm still startled when she stops at our table, her hips at my eye level in a scent of lemons.

The woman in the fur boots talks like a robot: "Excuse-me-sir-are-you-Levi-Dronyk-from-Beaverlodge-Alberta?"

"Sorry," I say. "Can't help you there, I'm afraid."

"Well-then-are-you-Jeff-Mieck-from-Tofino-British-Columbia?"

I glance at John Stark Lee and say, "No."

John Stark Lee says, "Hey Lady, you've been smoking too much crack."

She doesn't seem to hear John Stark Lee, stares at me only. Why is she staring at me so?

John Stark Lee says to me, "Dude, she's a robot."

And to the woman he says, "Uh yes, this is Jeff Mieck and he's wanted for MURDER ONE."

"Shut up, man," I tell him.

"I-must-contact-the-CIA," she confides calmly and walks away.

Everyone in the diner stares at us, not sure whose side they're on, citizens watching us warily over their Sprite on the rocks and coiled spaghetti and refills of acid coffee, and John Stark

Lee laughing spasmodically. The blotchy scar reddening on his chin and cheek where he steered his snowboard into the wrong trees, where a mountain branch entered his mouth, grey eyes open and laughing at himself, his stupid bleeding head stuck to the mountain. Like when a shrike impales a smaller bird on a buckthorn.

I look over, "Man, be quiet."

John Stark Lee laughs and shouts, "Hey Lady, I've got some crack cocaine for sale over here, do you want some?"

The woman walks to the payphone and picks it up without putting in any coins or dialing any numbers.

"Hello, is this the CIA?" she says into the phone. "Yes, I see Jeff Mieck and I am shivering in my boots with fear." She sounds almost sarcastic or teasing.

"Will you come down here and bring him in? We are at the diner."

She looks right at me.

"Oh no Jeff Mieck! Oh no Jeff Mieck! Jeff, you scare me!" There is something strangely sexual or theatrical in her voice; the woman sounds as if she's mocking me, as if she's flirting, answering some appetite.

"Oh Jeff, you scare me!"

"Oh my God," says John Stark Lee. "This is my first real psycho encounter. This has it all over TV. I'm so excited!"

"Shut up man."

I find myself wondering if she lives at the Red Planet Theatre, living and waiting for me behind the weird curtains where the big clean movie light used to flow straight across the room like a river in the air. I think about telling Bella when I get back.

"Hey lady! Are you Jeffrey Dahmer's mother? What did you say to Jeffrey when he kept going to the fridge?"

John Stark Lee does a squeaky impression of the Robot Woman's voice, almost crossing his eyes: "Son, if you open that fridge door one more time, heads are going to roll! Ha ha ha."

The woman leaves the phone and returns to her table. John Stark Lee keeps abusing her, though everyone is staring at him. A year back I would have joined in the joke. He notices a pretty younger woman looking at him. He settles down. Old people: who cares? Males his age: fuck them. Children: without clout. Pretty young women? Now this is an important category to John Stark Lee.

"Holy shit," he says to me in a lower voice. "What a total freak."

"Okay man, I think she's had enough abuse."

"Abuse? Calm down, man," he says.

"Well I'm just saying that —"

"No, you ain't saying nothing! You used to be all right, a bad ass, but now you're a wuss, coming back here with your earring, your fag tag, and your little answers. They got to you. Just like Bella. Both of you weird, fucking snobs and you think I can't see it."

"This is crazy."

"So it's crazy. Big fucking deal. You're the crazy one. Everyone else is crazy. Hey man, what's that say? Better go take Psych 100, Einstein."

We say nothing for a while. I try to finish my food in an uncomfortable silence. The morsels stand on my tongue and won't cooperate.

Melt of the Day. Kind of an ominous name really. Rinds of bright orange cheese that stretch like taffy, and under that layer either tuna or chicken or sauerkraut or massacred French toast. Someone made me something here in my home town. With their hands. I'm not too sure of the exact contents. My parents named me and always made me finish my food. The fast meal a living thing socked down in my stomach, fighting gravity and digestion.

"How's the burger?" I ask, attempting conversation. I lead with my chin. I am not the sharpest knife in the drawer.

"Oh it's just divine, *Jeff*. And hey, thanks for asking, *Jeff*."

We rise to leave our tense table as if at a border checkpoint. Still life with French fries. The CIA woman mutters something to me but I don't catch it all. "Jeff! Jeff!" she pleads lowly. A wallflower calling from the wall.

As we pass the payphone John Stark Lee grabs the receiver; he had this planned.

John Stark Lee glares right at the CIA woman and bellows, "I'd like to report a sighting of Jeff Mieck. Jeff's right here, but he's been taken prisoner by Robot Woman. I'm afraid it's too late. Jeff's one of them now"

John Stark Lee stares at me and laughs. I have to laugh too. He is a card.

But then my best friend hands the phone to me and walks out of Sneaky Pete's, walks hard like he's dragging a suitcase on wheels, disappears walking toward the wooden stores and curling river of ale and extinct snowy volcanoes and the scientists fenced off dinosaur relics: a buried race of kings, meat-eaters that could once run all the way to Patagonia.

Black payphone like a gun to my head I stand there, my feet disconnecting from the flat earth, getting air. The phone smells like vinegar and someone has said, I could fall for you in a big way.

In one ear the xylophone sound of the hushed hyper sea, wiring's hidden miles of copper intestines, and a jittery miniature city waiting at the end of the fibre optics, city and citizens waiting to be guided by voices, sprites, spooks. I discover I have nothing to say to the CIA. The metropolis's great boulevards and its night-map of tree branches that may one day enter your head.

I've gone away but John Stark Lee is the true nomad. Like the woman in fur boots, he is possessed, a life on the thorns.

I will fit in as a teflon clockwatcher, a studious clerk at the xerox machine, a denizen of hallways. I have this knowledge, this voice inside.

The woman in fur boots slips the phone from my hand, as if stealing, stealing me from a trance. She then holds onto my white hand and stares into my blue eyes, prepared to wait, prepared to grovel at my feet behind curtains. I am attempting to deserve the summons, her concentration of powers, the tempting weight of being chosen by the woman in fur boots.

The Scout's Lament

You're the GM, you bring in sixty bodies. But only twenty you want to see, I mean really look at.

The next twenty have a chance. Say you show them something they like. Say you're drilling holes in goalies. Knocking them down, a hot streak.

Then there are the last twenty. The last twenty are filler, warm bodies, keep a scrimmage going.

Now, do you know which twenty you are? You've GOT to find out.

Say the coach comes to your house, or a scout. Or maybe they don't come to your house. Get a feel. Phone them up. They treat you rotten you know that's how they'll treat your kid. You want your kid there? No you don't want your kid there.

Ask them what your kid should do for conditioning over the summer. *One,* this shows interest. *Two,* you see how they react, whether they could give a hoot. It's important. *Three.* I forget three. Go with your instincts.

And *Politics.* It's brutal. Some kid will make the team and you'll say WHAT THE HELL!? Whoa, whose nephew is that? It's really bad. And remember they get money for a draft choice from the NHL, so they're always looking at that. Factors. Certain traits they want, right or wrong. Some get pushed into steroids, get out the needles, bulk up, get in a 'roid rage, screw up their kidneys. They think it's their only chance at a barrel of cash and a hot car with local tarts crawling on it. Guys can't see past the end of their dick so they find someone at the gym can get 'roids and hypos. Backroom deals and politics like crazy. Not everyone's a star or a rocket scientist. Not everyone has a million choices.

Go to Portland, you walk in you're handed clean sweats, towel, the whole nine yards. You feel like a human. They phone, you listen. They got money and they'll spend it. Good food, good hotel.

The Cougars are a different can of worms. Cougars: bad food, bad rink, bad cans, housed poorly. Last year half of them got mono. No leadership. Coach of the week club.

They screwed kids on elegibility. Traded their best players to Kamloops.

No. Forget the Cougars. Go down to Cornell or Harvard, Notre Dame, Ivy League, or NCAA, do a degree, good degree, use your brain, play some hockey at the same time. It's impressive. You'll get invited anywhere after. Like Manderville with the Leafs.

You have to teach them something. Not just to brawl. Some of these guys, they are not kings and counsellors. Three time losers in nylon jackets. Gumchewers, can't organize a lay in a whorehouse with free labour. That coach we had here was too hard on them, knocking heads for no reason, pointless drills where they're getting injured, killing them, demolishing them; jeez they hated him.

Kent Manderville is a funny case. Told — not tough enough kid. His ma pulled him out. His ma. Now look, toughest on the team. Well maybe second or third toughest. College kid, Cornell, Ivy League, good degree, nice kid from Victoria, and now he's bashing and crashing with the Leafs. They want a berserker, make him into Curt Brackenbury. If he wants to stick. Same choice as when he was a kid. But he's not really like that. More a finesse guy. Maybe you get to like being a berserker. Never can tell. I still haven't learned to read minds. I tried though, tried to learn. I tried to read minds.

Some of these coaches got their certificate out of a Crackerjack box. You have to teach the kids *something*. You have to deal with kids' *heads*. Million miles from home, from their families. Fifteen, sixteen, they're *babies* really. Long road trips. Junk food. Blizzards, whiteouts, black ice all over the roads. Fall off the team bus with no legs and that instant you have to play some humungous farmboys waiting to knock your frigging block off. Things not going well. Bunch of strangers giving each other the greasy eyeball. Buses breaking down or going in the ditch on their side, like those Swift Current kids that died. Collecting stitches, broken noses, broken hands. The Philly flu. Psychology is a big thing. Some kids party like there's no tomorrow, go out and drink right after practice, boozehounds pissing it all away, soup to nuts. Or doing coke. They get a rep that's hard to ditch. And some kids just never fit in. What if your kid gets traded to Fernie, Podunk, Nowheresville? His best buddy gets cut from the club? What if your kid gets cut? They're out there, they're out there on their own, hung out to dry. It's hard on the kids. *Really* hard. You have to deal with kids' heads.

Lot of jerks out there too. Believe me. Lot of jerks. Guy here ran minor hockey and now in jail for molestation. I tried to punch his lights out in '69. I tried to take him out. Know what I mean? Guy hangs around injuries, all concerned. "Need sharper skates," he says to the kid. "Let me do them," he says. Bring them to your house. *Jeez.* Good service. Molesting eight- or nine-year-old boys on the hockey teams. Imagine what that did to their game, their love of the game.

You're asking. You're worried about your kid. It's *good* you're asking about this. Go with your instincts. There'll be tough times. I tell you no one but no one knows how hard it is to make it. Even to the minors or Europe. No one knows. We just see the guys that make it so we think no prob. Watch TV and think, I could do that. It's a long shot for anyone, no matter how good. I remember going through this. You're the skinny rookie, you're the new guy at camp they say to a veteran, *Run him.* See what you're made of. Tell the vet: run the new guy.

Maybe the new guy makes the team the vet doesn't. Blindside you in a scrimmage, cheap shot to the face. Try to get up he knocks you down. Creams you you spear him back, slit open his face, chop him upside the head — hey, no ref at a camp. No penalties. Other guy'll be pissed bigtime but coach'll be happy. He sees what you're made of. You go after the other guy no matter he's the size of a fucking ape. You can't back down. You must *retaliate.* Helluva thing but there you go. Carve him a new asshole need be. Dig down, find that old time religion.

I can give you a name — Tommy Black. Your kid'll have to join the Y. Tommy won't show him how to fight but how to defend himself. Nice guy. How to defend himself. Can't get away from it. Your skinny kid here goes into the corners he needs to worry about the puck, not the other guy. He needs to know he can take care of himself. Confidence is important to any athlete. Call Tommy Black. Firefighter, in great shape. Fifty-five and he looks half that. Friends with the Courtnall boys, coached them when they were kids. Went down to Los Angeles when the younger one married that movie star.

I've never been to Los Angeles. I've scouted for the Montreal Canadiens and the Whalers and some ragtag WHA outfits along the way. I knew Rocket Richard and Gordie Howe and his sons. I almost got on the same plane with Bill Barilko, yeah that one that crashed, and I've caught a lot of salmon over the years up in Campbell River. I shot a moose in Newfoundland and I've been treed by a grizzly in the Rockies. But I've never been to L.A. Seems kind of scary to me actually.

I know some tough young players in L.A. and they got mugged at a Wendy's. Knife to the heart. Maybe someday I'll get down see a game at the Duck Pond.

My boy was about twelve, small for his age. Gets levelled by a guy way bigger, knocked right on his can. But he springs right up and BAM BAM BAM! All over the guy. I was surprised, I didn't know he was like that. Little Tasmanian devil. You never really know.

Four years later some gorilla charges in full steam from the blue line — running him. My kid comes around behind the net with the puck, fast, BAM!! Into the boards. Then gloves off and drills my boy in the face going down. Brutal. Face a fucking mess. This time he didn't spring right up.

The needle moving through his cheek. I could read his mind this time.

My boy says to me while they're sewing up his face, "This isn't worth it. I don't like this game anymore."

He works with numbers now, an accountant. Handles money. Not a puck. He won't even watch hockey on TV anymore.

I watch. My job is to watch. I see a prospect I put in a word. Hope the big club will listen. Hope I'm right. I've sent them some good ones.

My boy had wheels too. Afterburners. And hands; make that puck get up and talk. Deke you in a phone booth. I still remember that needle and thread moving through his cheek. I don't like this game anymore, he says. And I still love it. Helluva thing.

But like I say, twenty get a legit look-see, twenty have an outside chance, and twenty are filler, nothing, losers.

Which are you? Which twenty are you right this moment? Do you ever know? Do you ever *really* know for sure? All my life. All my life I wonder this.

Love Is All Around Us

Once, the snow was so deep
you almost couldn't hear Margaret Atwood
—David McGimpsey

My close personal friend Kurt Waldheim phones me up —
lonely, everyone's ostracizing Kurt in his bunker aerie in Alberta's foothills, not as many Nazis as he thought. Can't I come
visit? Kurt's got a keg of Big Rock Traditional Ale and the new
Radiohead CD, some serious tuneage. Come on down, Kurt
says, come on down!

I hop the WestJet and Margaret Atwood is the stewardess,
Margaret Atwood pointing out the four emergency exits, Margaret Atwood asserting that no one has ever really seen those
plastic oxygen masks yet we cling to our belief that masks are
actually there, waiting for us like a parent, our Lacanian masks
waiting to drop.

Margaret Atwood says, Maybe my message is bleak because
it needs to be bleak. She says the seat-belt parts fit into each

21

other like a hook into an eye, my hook, your eye.

She lights a smoke, mutters, Screw the pilot and his feeble *No Smoking* light, it's a power issue, it's all political in nature. His phony blue uniform and dry-cleaning bills that could feed a third-world village. Her monotone voice rises: If a stewardess ceases to be critical, ceases to judge her world she'll find herself in one infinitely more turbulent.

I sigh and peer out the plane's tiny window, look down miles and see Margaret Atwood's giant face on the side of an orange United Farmers of Alberta grain elevator. Her giant face is live, mischievous, moving, gnomish. The elevator is like a drive-in movie screen. Her giant face winks largely at me, but then a double hook punctures her giant eye and the UFA elevator bursts into flame, rocketing burning timbers and burning grain across the street of the hamlet, grey charnel smoke enveloping the town and time going sideways under dead light from the stars.

Our stretch Avro Arrow touches down at Calgary airport. Inside the busy terminal we are greeted by Margaret Atwood in a cowboy hat. On the PA I hear Margaret Atwood's voice droning: *Mr. Burroughs to the white courtesy phone.*

Kurt picks me up in his coffee-coloured Mercedes and as we pull away from the curb I see her again, head shaven, Margaret Atwood dancing with the Hare Krishnas in a peach-coloured sarong.

Kurt takes me to the Ratskeller Klub for pilsner and blood sausage. Margaret Atwood climbs on the stage with a big twelve-string guitar and a Neil Young wig that looks to be made from the hair from a horse's mane or tail. She adjusts the mike, sings, *Hello Cowgirl in the sand, is this place at your command.*

Then kd lang leaps onstage with her Nancy Sinatra hairpiece and, holding hands, they belt out a bitching version of "These Boots Are Made for Walking." At the end of the song Margaret Atwood and kd lang hug, then start kissing like crazy, tongues and everything, whispering things into the mike like *Sleeping with a man is like being in a river but sleeping with a woman is the ocean.* Kurt Waldheim looks at me Kurtly while applauding politely. Atwood's husband Graeme Gibson snaps his fingers like a beatnik, but I suspect deep down he feels like Dennis Thatcher.

I duck out, check my messages: Margaret Atwood's recorded voice says, *You have no new voice mail; you have no new voice, male.* Message #2 is my mother asking, Why don't you write some nice Jungian ennui like that Margaret Atwood is so good at?

Then I'm chomping burnt rib-eye steak and drinking gin and tonic screwballs way up high in the revolving restaurant with Leon Trotsky and Don Cherry. Don is cracking us up with stories about Eddy Shore taking a cat-o'-nine-tails to him, until Leon Trotsky interrupts: Ach, it's that crazy woman again. I look out the window. Margaret Atwood is climbing the outside of the tower like King Kong, like Spiderwoman.

Don Cherry says, That Peggy! I tell ya! Great Canadian kid! Ya gotta love her! But I notice he tosses a twenty down and hightails it for the elevator.

A young woman peers out the window, says, We *did* her, we *did* Atwood, like last semester in, like, English 121.

Which book?

The Stone Angel.

That's one of her best ones. Totally.

Margaret Atwood smashes through the windows, lands on all fours in the broken glass, locks eyes, purrs to me, Love what you're doing with your hair, that Brian Eno-Howard DeVoto-male pattern baldness look. She kisses my bare scalp, leaving giant smears of red lipstick, says, Big party in Hal's Portuguese neighbourhood, we'll crash it. She spots Jan Wong eating, gets her in a headlock: *Let's do lunch. Tim Horton's, tomorrow. Noogie! Chinese haircut!* Jan Wong's glasses fall off, her hair askew and crackling static.

I sneak out with Don Cherry for shinny hockey at the rec centre. Margaret Atwood is the referee: striped jacket, scraggly effort at a ponytail. I'm on defence with Don. She drops the puck and Rocket Richard flies straight at me, his eyes lit like a Halloween skull. I can't even see where the puck is, try to stand him up, but he's like a bull; we all fall in a big pile of bodies and she blows the whistle, calls a penalty.

I assume the penalty's to me, but she says, *Rocket,* two minutes for looking so good. A riot starts in Montreal; Brador bottles and smoked meat sandwiches whiz past my skull.

Margaret Atwood places her powdered skull against mine, Atwood's sudden tongue like a pink hook in my ear.

Welcome to the bigs, she whispers. *May you live in interesting times.*

Another bottle slicing by my head. Can I think of a witty reply? I cannot.

Then Margaret Atwood is fading, a statue folded into a blizzard, she is sinking under the ice, she is going west on a jet. It's snowing and snowing; snow is general over Canada. Peggy! Peggy! we call from our wretched snowcaves, shivering, shrinking into our winter skin. Don't go! *Without you we are lost.*

Burn Man on a Texas Porch

Men who are unhappy, like men who
sleep badly, are always proud of the fact.
— Bertrand Russell

At fifty everyone has the face they deserve.
— George Orwell

Propane slept in the tank and propane leaked while I slept, blew the camper door off and split the tin walls where they met like shy strangers kissing, blew the camper door like a safe and I sprang from sleep into my new life on my feet in front of a befuddled crowd, my new life on fire, waking to *whoosh* and tourists' dull teenagers staring at my bent form trotting noisily in the campground with flames living on my calves and flames gathering and glittering on my shoulders (Cool, the teens think secretly), smoke like nausea in my stomach and me brimming with Catholic guilt, thinking, Now I've done it, and then thinking, Done what? What have I done?

Slept during the day with my face dreaming on a sudoral pillow near the end of the century and now my blue eyes are on fire.

I'm okay, okay, will be fine except I'm hoovering all the oxygen around me, and I'm burning like a circus poster, flames taking more and more of my shape — am I moving or are they? I am hooked into fire, I am hysterical light issuing beast noises in a world of smoke.

To run seems an answer. Wanting privacy, I run darkest dog-bane and daisies and doom palms, hearing bagpipes and whistling in my head, my fat burning like red wax, fat in the fire now Alone — I want to do this alone, get away from the others. I can't see, bounce off trees and parked cars, noise in my ears the whole time.

The other campers catch me and push me onto a tent the blue of a Chinese rug, try to smother me, but soon the tent is melting, merrily burning with me while everyone in the world throws picnic Kool-Aid and apple juice and Lucky Lager and Gatorade and ginger ale and ice cubes and icewater from the Styrofoam coolers. Tourists burn their hands trying to extinguish me.

My face feels like a million white hot rivets. I am yelling and writhing. One of my shoes burns happily by itself on the road. Where does my skin end and the skin of their melted tourist tent begin?

At some point in this year of our Lord I began to refer to myelf in third person, as a double: Burn Man enters the Royal Jubilee burn unit, Burn Man enters the saline painful sea. Burn Man reads every word of the local rag despite its numerous failings, listens to MC5 on vinyl, listens to Johnny Cash's best-known ballad.

I am not dealing with this well, the doctors tell me. I am not noble. They carried me in the burnt blue tent, a litter borne from battle, from defeat on the fields of fire and disassembly lines and into three months of shaking, bandaged pain. Your muscles go after you're burnt, but if you work out the skin grafts won't stretch over the larger muscles. Grafted skin is not as flexible as real skin. Skin is your cage.

Once straight, now I'm crooked. I lack a landscape that is mine. A doctor shone a light at the blood vessels living in the back of my retina. I saw there a trickle-down Mars in a map of my own blood: twin red planets lodged in my skull.

As a nerdy kid in horn-rimmed glasses, I haunted libraries, reading about doomed convoys in World War II, Canadian sailors burnt in the North Atlantic or off icy Russia, Canadian sailors alive but charred by crude oil burning all around them after U-boats from sunny Bordeaux took down their tramp freighter or seasick corvette — circular scalp of sea on fire and flaming crude races right at them, so eager, enters them, fricassees their lungs and face and hands, the burning ring of fire come to life on the Murmansk run.

I can't recall what happened when the burnt sailors moved back into the non-burnt world, crawled back home above Halifax's black snowy harbour or the sombre river firs of Red Deer, the saltbox houses of Esquimalt.

No war here; no peace either. Only the burn ward's manic protracted nurses sliding on waxed floors and the occasional distracted doctor with a crew of rookies whipping back the curtain, the gown, jabbing me to see if I'm done like dinner. Sell the sizzle. Door blows off the rented camper, spinning under sulphur sun, and I too am sent out into red rented sunlight, your basic moaning comet charging through a brilliantly petalled universe.

I was on a holiday in the sun, a rest from work, from tree spikers and salmon wars, from the acting deputy minister on the cellphone fuming about river rights, water diversions, and the botched contract with Alcan. I was getting away from it all, resting my eyes, my brain.

I had left the cellphone sitting like a plastic banana on the middle of my wide, Spartan desk. I was working on my tan, had a little boat tied up dockside, plastic oars, nine h.p., runs on gas-and-oil mix. I rested my skin on the sand-and-cigarette-butt beach. I lay down on a pillow in a tin camper. I caught fire, ran the dusty leaves and levees of our campground, alchemy and congress weighing on my mind.

Back home in my basement, a 1950s toy train circles track, its fricative steam locomotive emitting the only light in the room, swinging past where a slight woman in a parody of a nurse's uniform does something for Burn Man, for Burn Man is not burnt everywhere, still has some desires, and the woman doesn't have to touch anything else, doesn't have to see me, has almost no contact, has a verbal contract, an oral contract, say.

"Cindi: Yes that's me in the photo!" avows the ad in the weekly paper.

Cindi can't really see me, except for the toy-train light from my perfect childhood, can't make out my grave jerry-built face. I can barely see her. She has short, dark, hennaed hair that used to be another colour. I imagine her monochrome high-school photo. Dollars to doughnuts she had long hair parted in the middle, a plain face, a trace of acne. No one sensed then that Cindi would become an escort pulled out of the paper at random and lit by a moving toy train and red-and-yellow poppies waving at a big basement window — mumbling to me, I have these nightmares, every night these nightmares.

I explained my delicate situation on the phone — what I wanted, didn't want.

Good morning, Cindi, I said. Here's my story, you let me know what you think.

She coughed. Uh, I'm cool with that, she claimed.

So Cindi and I set up our first date.

My escort dresses as the nurse in white, her hands, her crisp uniform glowing in the rec room. All of us risk something, dress as something: ape, clown, worker, Cindi, citizen, *cool with that*

Here's an ad in *Now* magazine I didn't call: "FIRE & DE-SIRE , Sensuous Centrefold Girls, HOT Fall Specials, $150 per hour." I didn't call that number. I don't live in the metro area. I'm not one of the chosen.

Once, maybe, I was chosen, necking on the Hopper porch, that stunning lean of a Texas woman into my arms, my innocent face, our mouths one. Perfect height for each other and I am pulled to another doomed enterprise.

The iron train never stops, lights up my decent little town, its toy workers frozen in place with grim happy faces, light opening and closing them, workers with tin shovels, forklifts, painted faces. God gives you one face and you make yourselves another. My nurse is too thin. I like a little more flesh. I wish she'd change just for me.

My slight Nurse Wretched carries my cash carelessly and heads out to buy flaps of coke, or maybe today it's points of junk, for twenty or thirty dollars (her version of the stock market), delving into different receptor sites, alternate brands of orgasmic freeze and frisson, and she forgets about carrot juice and health food, any food, forgets about me, my eyes half-hooded like a grumpy cat's, eyes unfocused and my mouth turned down and our shared need for death without death, for petit mal, tender mercies.

Cindi is out this moment seeking a pharmacy's foreign voice and amnesiac hands and who can blame her?

Some people from my old school *(Be true to your school)* fried themselves over years and years, burned out over dissolute decades, creepy-crawling centuries.

Not me. Ten seconds and done, helter-skelter, hugger-mugger. Here's the new you handed to you in a camp ground like a platter of oysters. An "accelerant," as the firefighters enjoy saying, was used. Before I could change, had nine lives. Now I have one. O, I am ill at these numbers.

In the hospital not far from the campground I cracked jokes like delicate quail eggs: You can't fire me, I already quit. Then I quit cracking jokes. The skin grafts not what I had hoped for, didn't quite fit *(Why then we'll fit you)*. The surgeons made me look like a wharf rat, a malformed Missouri turtle, a post-mortem mummy. Years and doubt clinging to her, the nurse with the honed Andalusian face tried not to touch me too hard.

At first how positive I was! Eagerly I awaited the tray with the Jell-O and soup and fruit flies, the nurse with the determined Spanish face carrying it to my mechanical bed. I overheard her say to another nurse, No, he's not a bigot, he's a bigamist! Who? I wonder. Me? My aloof doctor? Does he have a life? If only we could duplicate the best parts and delete the rest. A complicated bed and her arms on a tray and her serious expression and unfucked-up skin and my hunger and love for a porch *(I spied a fair maiden)*, for the latest version of my lunatic past.

I spill Swedish and Russian vodka into my morning coffee now (rocket fuel for Rocket Man) and, blue bubble helmet happily hiding my scarred face, fling my Burn Man motorcycle with the ape-hanger handlebars down the wet island highway, hoping for fractious friction and the thrill of metal fatigue, hoping to meet someone traumatic, a ring of fire. I re-jetted the carburetor on my bike, went to Supertrapp pipes — wanting more horses and torque, wanting the machine to scream.

Before I became Burn Man, the Texas woman kissed me at the bottom of her lit yellow stairs, porch dark as tar, dark as sky, and her cozy form fast leaning against me, disturbing the hidden powers, ersatz cowboys upstairs drinking longnecks and blabbing over Gram Parsons and Emmylou *(One like you should be — miles and miles away from me),* impatient taxi waiting and waiting as we kissed. I had not expected her to kiss me, to teach me herself, her mouth and form, her warm image driven like a nail into my mind, her memory jammed on that loop of tape. (Such art of eyes I read in no books, my dark-star thoughts attending her day and night like a sacred priest with his relics.) In that instant I was changed.

Now I'm the clown outside Bed of Roses, the franchise flower shop beside the dentist's office on the road to Damascus, the road to Highway 61. On Saturdays I wave white gloves to passing cars — dark shark-like taxis, myopic headlights — and helium balloons with smiley faces bump my wrecked and now abandoned mouth. *(Where have all the old finned cars swum to?)* Pedestrians hate me, fear me; pedestrians edge past the busstop bench where the sidewalk is too narrow; pedestrians avoid my eyes, my psychedelic fright-wig. I want to reassure them: Hey dudes, I'm not a mime. Different union.

At Easter I'm a giant grey rabbit, but I can't do Santa. I could definitely use the do-re-mi but the beard isn't enough cover for my droopy right eye and melted cheek, the beard isn't enough to save face, and also I confess to trouble with the constant Ho Ho Ho.

Dignity is essential, I attempt to impart to a passing priest, but

I start coughing like a moron. *Drugs too,* I finally sputter. *Essential!* He moves on. Brother, sister, I may appear in ape costume at your apartment door, will deliver a singing telegram in a serviceable tenor. My grey rabbit suit needs a little bleach. Dignity is essential.

Burn Man must have his face covered, bases covered. I'm different animals. In the winter nights I'm the mascot Mighty Moose for our junior hockey team down at Memorial Arena. You may recall TV heads and columnists frowning on my bloody fight with the other team's Raving Raven mascot. All the skaters were scrapping, Gary Glitter's "Rock *&* Roll Part One" booming on the sound system, and then both goalies started throwing haymakers. I thought the mascots should also duke it out — a sense of symmetry and loyalty. I banged at the Old World armour of that raven's narrow, serious face, snapped his head back. Hoofs were my advantage.

Later we went for a drink or three and laughed about our fight, Raven and Moose at a small bar table comparing notes and bloody abrasions, hoofs and talons around each other, shop talk at the gin bin.

Don't fuck with me, rummy beard-jammers and balls-up bean-counters snarl at every bar on the island, as if they alone decide when they get fucked over. I could advise them on that. I didn't decide to have the camper blow to shrapnel with me curled inside like a ball-turret gunner.

They hunker down at the Commercial Hotel or Blue Peter Marina or Beehive Tap or Luna Lounge thinking they're deep, thinking one ugly room is the universe's centre because they're there with flaming drinks by the lost highway, clouds hanging like clocks over the Japanese coal ships and the coast-guard chopper, and across the water a distant town glittering the green colours of wine and traffic.

I sit and listen to their hyena patter, their thin sipping and brooding and laughing. Sometimes I'm still wearing my clown outfit while drinking my face off. Why take it off?

Friday night a man was kicked to death in this bar. In that instant, like me, he was changed, *his* memory jammed on a loop in a jar of wind, living the blues, dying.

At my front door a rhododendron sheds its scarlet bells one by one. A dark blue teacup sits on the rainy steps, looking beautiful and lonely, and there's a bird in the woods that sounds like a car trying to start.

One Sunday session a man lifted his golf shirt to show me his bowel-obstruction-surgery scar. His navel shoved four inches to the left. He didn't mind getting fucked over — in fact he guffawed gruffly at his own wrecked gut. We're so pliant, I thought, prone to melt, to metal, to a change of heart, to lend our tongue vows.

I who loved the status quo, liked things to stay the same even when they were bad. I who didn't want to break up with Dolly Varden girlfriends when it was obvious to everyone that we should get it over with. Then the camper door flies off: Kablooic! Goodbye Louie. I who loved the status quo.

I'm different animals now New careers in fire and oxygen, careering and hammering through the dolomite campground to fall on your tent, to fall on my sword. Home, I want to go home, darling. Take me back to Tulsa.

The skin is the largest organ; mine's a little out of tune. Your skin's square footage is — Jesus, how the hell should I know? Far more than your heart, which gets all the good press, attracts the spin doctors and diligent German scalpels.

Perhaps my Burn Man skin is more accurate now, what we all become after a certain age: parched animals, palimpsests in wrinkled uniforms, clowns hanging at the Pet Food Mart waving to the indifferent flow of traffic and shiny happy people.

I stare at a bottle of Ayinger German wheat beer, inhaling softest froth in my mouth, breathing in something good like a virus, like breathing oxygen and perfume with a woman's Norwegian hair all over your face.

I am The Way, I say to the drunken bottle, I am truth, heresy, *evidence* of what none of us wish to admit: that appearance is everything, that surface is God and God is surface.

Appearance: the white whale we chase every minute of every day. Looks and youth. We say this isn't so — Naysir, No Sir, No, No, No — we insist appearance counts for very little, but then I am walking at you, an ancient bog monster limping on the teensy sidewalk with my face like a TV jammed on the wrong channel, and at that sideways juncture ALL of us, ME included, decide shallow is not that bad. Let us, we decide, worship and grovel at the church of shallow.

Only Tuesday but I need a drink, my teeth caught in my

teeth. Down to the Starfish Room or Yukon Jack's, down to the sea in ships, hulls dragging on our city's concrete.

Flame created me with its sobering sound. Wake up, flame whispered in my ear, like a woman on a porch, like a muttering into cotton, a rush to action. It was ushering, acting on me, eating me. I'm its parent, I'm its home, and people worry they might catch it from me — catch ugliness, catch chaos theory, catch something catchy.

The baby doctor caught me when I came out in fluid, and my mother held me as a baby, such smooth baby skin, my skin dipped in baptismal water at St. John's, they washed away original sin, she held my perfect skin, my original skin. They lit fat candles in the cathedral and I came out in fluid in the university hospital.

The woman on the Texas porch said my skin was soft and that she loved my smell. No one ever said that before, and no one said it after. She created me.

As a kid I was burned by the summer sun in Penticton. My aunt from England peeled a section of skin from my back, and she still has that piece of my skin in a scrapbook in London.

Remember that map they torched at the beginning of each episode of *Bonanza?* I watched every week as a kid and when the flames came I thought, *neato-torpedo,* I thought, *cool.*

Where are my lost eyebrows? Did they fly up, up, up, or drift down as delicate ash, floating like some unformed haiku on a winter lake? My eyebrows got the fuck out of Dodge. Flames went up and down me as they pleased; fire didn't have to obey pecking order or stop-work orders. Kids in pyjamas watched me burn like Guy Fawkes, watched me dwell in possibilities. The doctor with zero bedside manner said the trick was simply to consider your face a convenience, not an ornament. Thanks for that, Doc. Maybe I could take a razor to him, see if he still debates function versus ornament after I've cut him a new face. Hate is everything they said it would be, and it waits for you like an airbag. You have to learn to deal with your anger, they said in the hospital. I am dealing with my anger, I'm dealing with my anger by hating people.

Here's a haiku I wrote in the hospital for the woman on the Hopper porch.

> Lawyers haunt my phosphorus forest
> I was bright paper burning in a glass gas-station ashtray
> Owning old cars is like phoning the dead

I might have to count the syllables on that baby — I believe haikus follow some Red Chinese system. The Texas woman plays a gold-top guitar, never played for me. She sings in a band doing Gram and Emmylou's heartbreaking harmonies. You narrow the universe to one person, knowing you cannot, knowing there's a price for that.

I want to be handsome more than anything else now that it's impossible, now that I'm impossibly unhandsome, and there is a certain hesitation to the nurse's step at my door, a gathering in of her courage, a white sun outside hitting her skin.

Before I caught fire in the campground I golfed with a

smoke-eater from Oregon. Mopping up after a forest fire he told me he found a man in full scuba gear lying on the burnt forest floor. Crushed yellow tanks, mask, black wetsuit, the whole nine yards. At first he thought it was a UFO alien or something like that. Scuba guy was dead. Recently dead.

They couldn't figure it out, how he got there. Finally some genius decided he must have been diving somewhere and a water bomber scooped him right out of the ocean and dumped startled scuba man onto the forest fire.

The smoke-eater from Oregon on the golf course swore this was a true story, but then I'm in England, a little seaside cottage in ugly Essex, my Thatcherite uncle snoring, and what starts off this American cop show on the telly? A TV detective talking about this scuba diver found in a forest fire. Then a month later a neighbour I bumped into at 7-Eleven insists it actually happened to him on Vancouver Island near Central Lake by Port Alberni. Water bomber scooped the diver out of the big lake, not the ocean. Now I don't know what to believe. Everyone keeps telling me the same false true stories.

The toy train runs and Cindi shows me a photo of herself as a little girl in a little bathing suit at the beach *(Yes that's me in the photo!)*.

Cindi cries, points at the photo: Look. I look so happy! Once she was happy. Now she has nightmares. Cindi lights a cigarette, says she wants to see real icebergs and lighthouses before she dies. Then she says, I dreamed the two of us travelled to Newfoundland together, and it was so nice and calm; not one of my nightmares. Cindi also dreamed I killed her. She says, When I die, no one will remember me, and tells me it must be her period coming on, makes her emotional. I decide mixed messages may be better than no messages at all, though I feel like the palace eunuch.

Cindi spends half her day looking for matches. Cindi struggles with her cigarette, as if it takes great planning to get face to end of cigarette; she seems to move her face rather than move the cigarette. Cindi says, Nothing attracts police like one headlight. *Do you know why I pulled you over?*

At the tavern by the rushing river, men said things to me in my clown suit, my eunuch suit, thinking they were funny. They were deep. The waitress knew me from my previous life, gave me red quarters for the jukebox. She trusted my taste, trusted me once at her apartment. She wore deliberately ugly plaid pants and her wise face looked just like the Statue of Liberty's. With the bar's red quarters I plugged honky-tonk and swing B-sides only. The B-sides rang out, sang their night code to me alone: Texas, kiss, lit stairs, a world changed.

The old boys in the Commercial Hotel had been drinking porch-climber, watered down shots of hooch, emptying their pants pockets, their bristle heads.

We watched a man kicked directly to death. Strangely, it was an off-duty police officer who had stopped another officer for drinking and driving and refused to let him off. The drunk driver was suspended from the force, from his life. Then guess who humps into whom at the wrong bar?

The night alive with animals, the whole middle-class group taking some joy in the royal beating, displaying longing, bughouse excitement, wanting to get their feet in like mules kicking, believing it the right thing to do. He was struggling. I don't think they meant to kill the policeman with their feet, but it was a giddy murder, a toy in blood. They busted his head and eyes and busted his ribs and arms and kidney and returned to their drinks, expecting him to resurrect himself on his own power with his swollen brain and internal bleeding. Then the ambulance attempting to dispense miracles, a syringe quivering into muscle. It was fast. I stood fast. I stood shaking in my suffocating clown suit and they returned to their drinks and sweaty hyena hollering, their *Don't fuck with me, Jack,* their legions and lesions and lessons and their memories of twitching creations face down in the parking lots of our nation.

I can wait. Wait until they pass out, then punch a small hole in the drywall under the electrical panel and pour in kerosene, my accelerant du jour. I will run before the doors blow off. See how they like it. See how they like Cindi and the Spanish nurse's Flamazine lotion. It's basic pysch. You want everyone else to have the same thing you caught.

Nothing happens, though, because I feel immediately moronic and melodramatic, dial 911 outside, and firefighters are on top of it lickety-split. The doors don't blow, their faces don't fry or turn to wax. I fly away on my rare Indian motorcycle with a transplanted shovelhead engine and Screamin' Eagle calibration kit. No one new joins my Burn Man Club. Burn Man is alive and the unyielding moral policeman is dead, his family in dark glasses at the bright graveyard.

Oh, how our sun smiled on me, breezes blew softly in the dappled leaves over the low-rent beach and my head touching a cool pillow. I napped and the propane fire snapped my skin, remapped me. I twisted and travelled in beautiful lost towns and low registers of postmodern western wind from the Sand Hills of Saskatchewan.

I am a product of light, of hope.

I still have that shy desire for the right fire to twist me back just as easily to what was: to milky youth and a mysterious person falling toward me on a Texas porch with her tongue rearranging hope in my mouth. Under oak trees by the river the Texas woman put words in my mouth, secret words pushed in my mouth like a harmonica. *Her temple fayre is built within my mind.* Perhaps God will have mercy on me in my new exile.

The right fire. Doesn't that make sense?

Like corny cartoons and television shows — amnesia victim loses memory from blow to head, but a second blow makes it right, fixes it all right up, no matter what.

I remember a relevant episode of *I Love Lucy.* Ricky Ricardo's memory pops back after Lucy hits him by the fireplace: Ricky comes swinging back, I come back, my old skin swims back from its minor shipwreck, from the singing sirens, the torpedo, finds the muscle memory held like a Rolodex in my new skin.

Doesn't seem to work. Can't buy pointed boots back from a swollen brain, can't drift again into your childhood face or her blue truck and blue eyes and blond hair and stories of west Texas waltzes and Cotton-Eyed Joe. Can't saw sawdust.

Instead I rise Saturday a.m. with TV cartoons, set up a supper-time date with Cindi — God bless her, at least she takes me, takes me as I am (Yes that's *not* me in the photo) — Burn Man climbs inside mask and clown suit like a scuba diver, like Iago on Prozac. For what seems a fucking century we wave white gloves at you *(Drowning not waving),* wave at blind drivers passing Bed of Roses and the helium balloons — gorgeous ivory moons and red planets bump-bumping my skin, trying to enter the hide of Burn Man's teeming serious face, trying to push past something difficult and lewd.

Ours really is an amazing world. Tristan falls in love on a Hopper porch, but Isolde loses faith in a Safeway parking lot, Isolde takes the magic bell off the dog. And a famous scuba diver rockets like a lost dark god into smoking stands of Douglas fir, into black chimneys burning.

Song from Under the Floorboards

I go about 190. I'm down in the pit and you drive over me, wait for me to do it. I'm broadminded, but sometimes my head just hurts and hurts. I hope it's not the years living with hydro-carbons and monoxide.

I hope it's not anything serious (meaning I hope it's *comic?*). In high school I was thirty pounds less but who wasn't? Toting our thirty-pound sack: now that alone should be dandy exercise. *Logically,* you think, flesh should defeat itself just from lugging it about a decade or two.

There is no convincing *logic* in my life. In high school I am shy and they decide I am stuck up. I got in a little trouble, hated the sabre-rattling coaches, though they were just humans trying to get the job done with a herd of hormonal cutups.

As running back or wide-out I couldn't make first string, but an assistant coach with a cueball head and a Texas-Saskatche-wan accent converted me into a deadly defensive back. Found my niche. Big white numbers painted into the grass under our cleats, rows of zeroes and our uniforms glowing like phosphorus, like pillars of salt, and I liked how I looked in shoulder pads at night, my long hair sticking out of the helmet, gold bolts of neon lightning licking our midnight blue helmets.

How I loved to submarine someone cocky from a rich school in the west end, take out their knees and flip them onto the rock hard earth behind our purple brick school, flip them like a burger and make them mortal.

The big lights painful to stare into, the wider black sky and six white suns set on each stanchion, shifting halos and coronas and sunspot flares. So much bleached light pouring down on our playground, our lonely glowing squad.

God I could run and cut like a damn cat and I didn't need to catch a thing: just bat the ball down or torpedo them exactly as the pigskin arrived.

Some voice in my ear like Captain Beefheart singing "Willie the Pimp" and the voice always right.

He's going long, it's obvious.
Buttonhook this time, watch out for the mondo fake.
Fast slant, QB thinks he's Tom Wilkinson, trying to
munch us a few yards at a time.

I was no star and I dated no cheerleaders but I danced backwards with a voice there like a dog at a gramophone, like a microphone screwed in my skull; plant a cleat and change and charge, polished helmet lowered smack into the receiver's floating thighs and he cartwheels, pigskin flying loose into space in slow motion, and now down in a pit I do lube and oil and differential and I slap econo mufflers onto econo cars with a little greasecap on my head like a miniature fez and that speedy special voice gone AWOL, lost in the stars, no more Captain Beefheart voice telling me what to watch for in my econo life, just the sign STOP Please Wait for Attendant and a trouble light hanging.

White smoking klieg lights hung over the high school field; red and green strobes washing the blues band on the high school stage. We smoked up walking to the winter dance, laughing in the snowy laneway, jostling, pay the cover, big Har Har Har at the milling steamy entrance, but on the gymnasium dancefloor I felt less sure, a child bride of sorts, prepared to dwell in possibilities but suddenly sure that females sensed unknown failings in me. Paula looked so pessimistic and fetching that one winter dance but I could not put a sentence together.

She was serious, brainy, disapproved of me not being able to put a sentence together. I knew she knew the word hippocampus. On the dancefloor I seized up, stopped dancing completely and she stared at my paralysis, and I fled out the alarmed doors, red bells and hammers smashing, crowd panic, and then the girls definitely sensed some failing in me. My high school years breathed disappointment, fear, white noise. One thing did not lead to another.

Everyman's Tonto or Alice B. Toklas or Angus Park Blues Band grinding it out onstage, distorted psychedelic bands I loved, but the *voice* failed me on the dancefloor, the voice didn't tell me how to move at the stoned Sadie Hawkins dance. I always did the wrong thing, uttered the wrong syllables, and these wrong things blew my chances. Why do very tiny events make me question organized religion or the actual width of a wonky life? Still, I never pulled a trigger. I'm waiting, waiting for the attendant.

I try to be smarter as an older person, try to make up for how stupid I was, try to stay awake after sex, that beautiful performance, to stay awake whispering sweet nothings as a sensitive Redford might in a putrid romance flick, but God or some very convincing authority figure hits a switch that basically says, Slim, your current onboard DNA and sorry salt of the earth brainstem inclinations really lean toward deep primitive sleep now I do apologize about that.

Hating school I stayed an extra year just to play ball in that phosphorus uniform the colour of some trendy cocktail. Hated school and stayed extra. I'm a fool for ball though I haven't played now for, oh, several years.

Two friends, guys I liked, killed themselves while attending my purple high school. I was surprised by the suicides, saw no "signs," though it's safe to say I was too wrapped up in my own complaints to be aware of anyone else's obtuse smoke signals. Both friends liked smoking dope. Jack Gaines in my biology class had long hair like me, acne riding his face, and a big calm grin like a wolf, a stoned wolf. Twenty years ago. Does anyone else remember Jack and his wolf grin? I can't remember much else but at least I remember something (I remember that we smoked a lot of dope before I quit because of the paranoia that sent me running from parties).

Jack Gaines and I joked around a lot in Biology 20, gabbing, not really paying attention, though we liked the biology teacher who drove a cool Mercury from a year like 1947 or 1953. I didn't see Jack much outside of that biology class. The teacher we liked was fired. If we thought the teacher was good, then the school board thought he was bad.

Hey I could make a whack of dough just betting against myself.

This McLube must sit on the tiniest piece of real estate downtown, corner of two main drags, world spins by and tiny dust devils in the parking lot, like the dust devils in the old playground, dust devils in the schoolyard. Memories move across your head like head lice did in that childhood classroom (thought Miss Sampson said someone had *headlights*).

Two suicides but I don't remember two funerals. Suicides were hush-hush then. The papers would say, Joe Blow died *suddenly*. I bet they both thought the world would be sorry, the world would miss them now. Does the world miss them? Is the world sorry? Do those naked bald mannequins in the store window sense the streamlined future first? Mannequins already live there with their unblinking marble eyes and lack of high school blemishes, mannequins like suicides, alone in the many blue futures.

Was Jack's acne a factor, a reason to snuff yourself? In high school, acne walked over my back and chest, but my acne was secret acne and Jack's acne was public acne, his acne was testifying, out in the open, his red flag. He saw skin doctors, he ruined pores on his face dabbing on too much drugstore alcohol.

Jack Gaines sat in a Pontiac with another guy listening to radio music as the Detroit engine purred in a closed garage, sleepy, you're getting sleepy, carbon monoxide changing their skin to a healthy reddish-pink, tiny new riders kicking into their crowded bloodstream.

Cars pull in over my pit and they shut the motor down, try to spare me from monoxide. I wonder if the car radio played crap or something good like Cream or Tull, some good wah-wah pedals and Leslie speakers. I wondered why Jack was sitting with another guy. Did that mean something, dying with a guy? Not exactly Romeo and Juliet. Maybe it was a stoned error; maybe Jack just turns over the Pontiac's Slant-6 mill so he doesn't wear down his dad's battery, so the 'rents don't yell at him, the parents who will find them, engine warmed up, bodies going cool. Carboxyhemoglobin concentration of 91 percent in blood, the post-mortem pathology report tells the parents.

Down in my pit I open four litres of 10-30 and oil flows like beautiful honey while women drivers linger in cars above me, long legs and my sure hands calling forth slick fluids. My face and fingers so close to their legs, their warm *loins*. They come and go. Women pay. The car shudders like a live animal. A game of inches but they might as well pass miles overhead in a supersonic jet. I'm groundcrew in a high tech tomb, voice muffled in a muffler shop. They shut off their motor.

I put my head back on my neck and stare straight up through steel floorboards at women nestled (the cosy nest they carry about themselves) up there breathing on milky coffee and a complimentary copy of the *Globe*.

Women worry about their car. Their white blouses are so clean. My hands are filthy. They're always buying impressive underwear and chairs. They pay. Customers turn into pieces of paper; blow away like a voice. Women wonder if their boyfriends love them, they're sure the Atlas moving men with panther tattoos stole something. I'm deep under their blue Polaroid city, the virtual reality village we stroll through in our head, our hippocampus route map.

I knew a woman who moved to this city from the Badlands and she couldn't believe how white all the men's hands were. She was used to coyotes and miles of fissured land, hands with dark oil and grease ground into lines and under and around the nails, hands working over truck and tractor engines, grime never coming out. At the farm and at the tiny Badlands school house these altered hands moved around her, moved over her clean blouses and impressive underwear like magpie shadows, travelled inside her, altered her.

My hands are a crosshatched mess; I check your transaxle level, your U-joints and PCV, I'm your underground greasemonkey in a boiler suit, your monkey man doing the same task over and over. Crazy crows look identical in every city. I know the smell of new cardboard boxes and rubber mats. When was the last time I saw a bluebird roving a skeleton forest? Let's just say on occasion the bluebird of happiness morphs into a heat-seeking missile and you're trying to stay one step ahead, keep it from zooming up your exhaust pipe.

Gram Vincent, suicide #2 from my class, had wit and charm to spare and black hair in a nice Beach Boys cut; he had a lopsided sarcastic smile and an elegant shotgun in his parents' basement. Why attack the head, attack yourself? His ornate shotgun looked like it might utter witty Ivy League bon mots, but it clawed a section of his head away lickety-split. Gram always seemed to be laughing at some private joke while talking with you about mundane things. Gram and I never talked shotguns. Of course we never talked mufflers or crappy jobs either. What did we talk about?

Gram was an interesting guy but the shell's lead pellets expanded outward in a cone shape and cut that exact shape out of the front of his face, and at that point Gram was no longer an interesting guy. Do you change your mind at the last second, when the lead pellets are already released?

Grim Gram was down in the basement mixing up the medicine: Gram became a song from under the floorboards, a message waiting for his mother trotting down the stairs to find, to see some of his brain stuck on the wood panelling. The gun in your hand rattling like a seedpod and the head with the Beach Boys haircut waiting.

I don't get sentimental about Gram's suicide yet I do about Jack Gaines's. What's the difference? I can't figure it out. Gram's death with a shotgun took more courage. Your trigger finger versus a familiar key turning in the ignition. A car key is easier, more gradual than a shotgun's exact trigger, but that doesn't sway me, doesn't cut the mustard now twenty years later. I think about Jack Gaines in his car.

I stuck around. Hated school but stayed where I was. Now I'm down in the snakepit trying to make sense of things. You drive in over top. I'm the person under you. *Wait for the Attendant,* the sign says.

You're in a hurry, you're on top, you're glad you're not down in the hole. I remember Jack and Gram in the hall grinning, laughing, joking.

Playing ball I could run, run amuck, run smack into any guy on the field but we guys never asked each other anything that was important. Guys find about two things safe to talk about. No one talks shotgun itch or sincere worries or mystery grievances. Maybe Jack and the mystery guy in the car talked. The muffler shop radio serves up classic rock: Aerosmith, Petty, the Stones. All *lame.* Why play the Stones and their prepackaged predictable version of sin and death? The second album with "Down Home Girl" and "Little Red Rooster," okay; 196s, okay. But now the Stones put their teeth in and flog fake sin like a shoddy wristwatch in a Woolco parking lot and everyone shells out for nosebleed seats in the arena. The haunted Louvin Brothers or any owly 1950s bluegrass band knew more about sin and death.

I didn't go to your school. I went to that school across town with the weird name and purple bricks and new design with no windows. They filled in the yellow swamp, the cattails and hidden birds, the pasture at the edge of town, the horse with cow sense, and the calves with screwworms.

You knew no one from that school but your coach said, Keep your head up boyos. Your coach said, Watch that sumbitch defensive back with the faggy long hair submarines my best goddam receivers.

In memory Jack Gaines's garage becomes our garage; I see Dad's car purring, our family's wooden toboggan hanging in the rafters; I hear a good car radio playing, notes hanging in the exhaust, radio playing on, but no one listening after a while.

Outside the garage winter stars and northern lights crackle over tapered snowdrifts in the backyard. As kids we blasted through the icy crust to crawl inside those soft snowbanks. Our old cat tried to walk across the crust and fell into a different world.

Jar those pretty boys from the other side of town and they think twice before drifting across the middle, before taking flight like an angel in Sport Chek cleats. Horses and calves stood here. Crimson players scramble swiftly off the line, a herd rumbling on hard ground, trying a pick play, but they don't fool me.

Over and over a football leaves the quarterback's hand. Gangly receivers crisscross, look back for a ball. We float in night sky to meet, strangers under stanchions of blinding lights, and I hit like a mock sparrow-hawk, knock them out of *my* sky, down into the pit.

Your coach put a $50 bounty on my head but that made me play better. He was giving me valuable coupons, put methanol in me, rocket fuel.

1973. I float, a low SAM missile set loose by the Viet Cong, miles to roam and no one can touch me. I'm not even twenty-one. I am what, maybe seventeen, eighteen.... For a while I am free, that voice jammed in my head like a high heel on a dancefloor.

Eskimo Blue Day

After my two boys finish their lesson, I let them splash in the shallow pool, everyone in goggles, vaguely insectoid. A rip in my four-year-old's plaid trunks and his tiny bum reveals itself, which makes us chuckle. My boys have their fun in the water while I read at a row of patio tables pierced by large floral umbrellas (they expect rain *inside* this municipal building?).

I glance up from my magazine. Little Jeremy is in trouble: head back, small mouth open, and he is sinking and rising, he can't keep his head up.

I leap the tiny plastic fence and potted plants to help my youngest son (he has a rip in his plaid trunks and his tiny burn shows). I will lunge into the pool in my best worsted suit and wool tie — no compunction. My youngest boy is drowning, but I will save him and he will love me and we will be happy forever and ever.

I land on the other side of the tiny ornament of a fence. Tiles, a small plastic drain. My foot hits a pool of water, my foot travels on, and I crash blue tiles: hips, spine, shoulders, then snapping my head back and my head smashes wet tiles, my head rings like a bronze bell. I know my skull cracks open — choice secrets vanish from the colliculi, pages yanked from the cerebral cortex. My bone gourd cracks like a hollow ceramic pot from Value Village.

The standard cartoon version of this humiliation is reasonably accurate — stars and planets — and it's so fast, my two eyes full of vile virile light, like gazing into a scarlet traffic light an inch away. An accident, an excited crowd gathering around my spectacular but ordinary pool of blood which finds its speechless way to the plastic drain, and I feel ashamed for being injured, for being impolite, for bleeding. I know I am in the recreation centre, but I can't remember what I am recreating.

My boy in the water, I say clearly through a mouth brimming with strange syrup.

What's he saying?

You okay, Mister?

Jeez that blood's really gushing out of there.

It's a regular fountain.

My boy, I try to repeat. *The water!*

He wants some water. Is that okay? Can he have a glass of water?

Man, he really did a number on his head. Did you *hear* it? PLONK!

That blood is a veritable fucking fountain.

I think we've covered that topic, I attempt to interject.

Loosen his collar button.

Don't move him. Or maybe turn him on his side.

My boy, I insist.

Shouldn't be running by the pool you know.

My teeth taste of blood, salt, sea sounds, motorboat noises, vrooom, var-ooom, captain hats, childhood lake noises echoing in my broken head, woodpeckers with their specially designed sponge skulls knocking cottonwood trees over our barefoot walk up to the cedar cabin's iron bunkbeds and wet bathing suits that stick to your cold skin, your nuts cold, suit still cold when you draw it on your hips to enter water once more. I love my dead mythic past, my dead father, love my flawed skull, the way it used to be, some fine article half-hidden in the produce section.

The lank lifeguard is half my age, a tall redhead in a blue tanktop and black shorts. He towers above. His skull is still intact.

I know First Aid, he announces.

He bends over like a freckled hinge, a thin leather string around his neck. He peers in my eyes, places a cold thumb on each of my eyelids and I think of the Eucharist, my eyes moving like nervous Jell-O and my youngest boy living under clear city water, my youngest boy down in the blue pool with ripped plaid shorts and on blue tiles a crowd gazing at me like I'm their latest model Trinitron, crowd looking at the wrong squished spider.

Oh my bloody head, placing streaks and dots in the air, messenger with no message, my less-than-impressive agony. I'm getting the new specs, the modifications. Tell it to stop changing channels. My eye moving to the water, a wall laid flat. In Kipling's World War I story the gardener in the French cemetery says to the woman, *Come with me and I will show you where your son lies.*

Hey, you'll be okay, the lifeguard says. Heads bleed a lot, he says. They always look worse than they are.

From beside the pool I can see the weight room, jaunty men behind glass trodding treadmills, men walking out over the water in pool reflections and glass panes the colour of icebergs and fluorescent light. They step over noisy seas to my son.

My son hears a black piano, thunder under water. One man cranks a red button on the treadmill — he will arrive faster. Our invisible sons, our hidden faith under floral umbrellas (and no storm inside here) — our almost-lost hopes nattering at us like a coalition government.

The thumb on my eyelid and my eye moving to the water. Where else in the world to go? What else but try to rise?

Skin a Flea for Hide and Tallow

I never want to leave this country;
all my relatives are lying here in the ground,
and when I fall to pieces I am going to fall to pieces here.
Shunkaha Napin (Wolf Necklace)

Schultz and the drunken Orangemen chased me out of Fort Garry with horsewhips and bayonets. I lit out for Pembina and St Joseph, worked as a scarecrow gravedigger down around Fort Snelling and Sacred Heart Settlement.

Dig graves or starve. I could have eaten a folded tarp. I dug dirt for six years and now six seasons later I'm in a blue uniform riding into Montana Territory with that horse's ass Custer and a thousand arrows coming at me. Men I ate pork with last night twitch strangely on the ground and Brûlé children try to kill me in a thicket, laughing at me. More damn graves for someone to dig. Flint arrowheads and cut-tin arrowheads break bones, open in you like a flower. Tin arrowheads are the worst.

After the bitter bad Sioux raids we moved warily on the troubled road between pillars of smoke to bury anyone we stumbled on. Could not tell sometimes if they were white or otherwise, bodies stripped and heads mangled or cut off or eyes scooped out with horn spoons. It takes a long time to bury a dozen or two dozen bodies, to dig holes for whole German or Norwegian families. Their pets or animals we threw into the high grass or into lakes with weights.

None of us on the side of angels. Both sides plunder and rape and both sides kill children *(nits make lice)*. Both sides scalp, especially the escaped convicts and Missouri bushwhackers and veterans of the war between the States; they are tough old dogs with knives hidden and nothing in life spooks them anymore.

The hangman was happy to hang dozens of Indians, charcoal and pigment still smeared on their faces; happy to hang almost anyone since Sioux had recently killed all of his children and his young wife.

I saw the merchant John Bozeman and his freighters and scouts killed by strange roving Blackfeet on his own road to Virginia City, the Powder River trail, the Bozeman trail, John Bozeman killed on the trail named after him, killed by his prosperity and industry in fur and gold. Sioux and Blackfeet didn't want him barging through the choicest parts of their beautiful country. They'd already seen it happen.

I could tell John Bozeman something about that, about losing my country.

The Orangemen with bayonets and horsewhips made me flee Fort Garry up in Canada, made me leave my family behind. The Ontario volunteers and the Schultz faction tried to kill me in the river with rocks. Goulet was murdered, murdered as if we were the intruders.

They chased Fenians and Métis and hillsiders, chased anyone they didn't like the look of. Guilmette was murdered, they shot a priest, bayoneted Nault. They drank the country dry looking for wagon men to stab or shoot or beat or turn in for a reward, bothering poor Louis Riel's mother, turning her little house upside down every few days, in case her son was hiding there in a kitchen drawer.

A man back in Toronto was offering $5000 for Riel's head in a sack and any number of Christian razors wanted to collect.

I lived in Minnesota for about three years, then drifted west to Nebraska, along the shores of the Platte, and up to Deadwood with a shifty outfit of wolfers and reeking hide and bone men, teamsters and whiskey-traders following more rumours of gold and all of us hungry men, all of us hungry. The government was about to open up the Indian Territory, so let's get there first, right?

In talk by the tents and night firelight it comes out that I am a gravedigger by trade, and then the look in a fire-lit eye changes, every time, as if I am sizing them up for a coffin or a shroud, which I am not.

Now Indians in broken eyeglasses and with buffalo blood streaked on their cheeks are sizing me up, trying to provide me with a military funeral in the valley dust and sage and wild rose and crabapple. Is this my grave? Why then I'll fit ye, they seem to say. All this coming down on my skull because there were no jobs after the Panic of '73. I was skint, clawing wild bulbs and turnips out of the ground, scrounging coal left along the railroad. I was lousy, starving; but to think I asked to do this, to ride with Iron Butt Custer.

My cavalry horse was hungry and half dead when I finally shot the nag so I could burrow behind the hot belly and shoot savage nations and Jackie Lyons beside me doing the same behind his horse.

In the morning we rode down the ridge, down the slanting earth, and dismounted briefly, but Dreamers and dog soldiers roared at us like a threshing machine and we mounted again and climbed back up the ridge in a mad race, there to dismount once more. A cursed place to make a stand, no cover at all. What was Iron Butt thinking? Goes to West Point and all he knows how to do is charge and chase women, white or red. Damn your eyes, I swore, knowing my luck was running muddy, knowing we were bogged to our saddle skirts, Christ to be dead, and to know that, brain before the body.

One young soldier couldn't stop his spooked horse and it took him into the Indians, his horse's head out low and his head leaning back trying to turn the plug. How do you hide from five thousand Indians? Their tiny wild horses snapping like ugly dogs, savages lining up in the dust to get a chance at us, taking turns, more of them than there are fiddlers in hell. You'd need wings to get away.

I joined the U.S. Army with a false name because in 1875

they were taking anyone who could walk and chew gum. They didn't give a hoot. March green recruits around a sunny parade ground for a few days and issue rifles and let us hunt after Lo the Indian. Immigrants with no words of English, and ragtag ne'er do wells like me, seeking an army blanket and maggoty crackers and pocket money, though they never pay us when we're near a town with a bottle of tonsil varnish or a whore to lie with. I know how to ride and shoot from summers hunting bison with Gabriel Dumont but many recruits do not know a muzzle from a pizzle. I wish Gabriel and some others were riding with me.

Iron Butt Custer is supposed to be a sharpshooter but Bloody Knife joked that he couldn't hit the inside of a tent. I saw Custer shooting chukar in the Black Hills, though, and he looked a good shot. We were not supposed to be in the Black Hills. Looking for gold. This was asking for it. We found human skulls and a Canadian penny and cave drawings of strange animals and ships. Custer cut off all his long hair for the summer heat and dirt and vermin; Custer took metal horse clippers to his head; maybe Iron Butt cut into his good luck when he cut his hair. Hurrah, we've got them, the jackass Iron Butt said in the morning when he saw the circles of the huge village through the Austrian field glasses. Painted Nakota, Santee, Cheyenne, Blackfeet, Oglalas, Unkpapas in their peltry lodges, singing like dry axles. Custer scribbles a message and gives it to the Italian, Martini.

Is the man blind or poxy in the head? Jackie Lyons sputters. He'll have us all killed! Does he not see this coming on us and does he not care?

The papists and ex-papists among us crossing themselves, smelling brimstone and buck-horn handled knives.

Three Crow scouts melted away after they noted the brevet general wanted to attack. No one can call what we did an attack. Rifles jamming from dirty ammunition and arrows rattling down and I am thinking, Blast me, if these savages don't kill the ghostly blond fop I swear I will. Thinks he's so lucky that he can do anything, ride into hell's half acre with a few fop cousins and his pretty gilt hairbrush.

I'll crawl over F Company on my belly with a hatchet and kill Custer if the Indians haven't. Put a window in his skull. That would be a good trick: kill Custer and not be able to tell anyone I was the murderer.

Minutes or hours I have been lying on my stomach with five others in a circle, our heels touching. Marched half the fecking night for this, no sleep, bloodshot half-blind eyes, grumbling at each other on our dog-tired nags, nags hungry and trying to eat grass right until we shot them behind the soft ear.

Some lost their horses, and I still see the men trying to hold their horses' reins, boots wide, arms out and pulled, twisted, unable to stand and hold their reins in the mayhem.

I wanted to run when my companion Jackie Lyons took an arrow exactly in the spine — it sounded like it hit brick or wood and lodged there as he screamed out, as he reached around and touched the shaft and tried to yank it out of his backbone. Legs dead, face not his face at all, grey as his shirt.

Jackie's screaming does not aid my nerves.

A 16-shot Henry rifle and a Spencer carbine are firing to the north of us and I shoot over my poor skewbald horse until my rifle jams. I hit one savage with a shot right in the mouth and a goodly portion of his lower jaw flies away. He is wearing porcupine quills and a weasel tail. He has smallpox scars. This particular cut-throat does not fall but walks away from me without a chin, walks away as if he just recalled an appointment elsewhere. I don't know if I have killed any of the pirates. We seem to have little effect and they are merry as crickets.

Every few moments I look back at Jackie Lyons but I can't help him now, I have to watch the slope below us.

I tried to pull the arrow's shaft but the tendon tied at the top of the shaft gave way and the arrowhead remained driven into poor Jackie's back in sweat and blood. I get my knife out, not for his back but to clear my jammed rifle. Something wrong with the ammunition or rifles. Spent shells won't pop out, making it hard to shoot more than once. These cursed Yankee rifles. I want to scream. We had better weapons with Riel in Fort Garry six years ago.

I'm sputtering and crawling around for another rifle when Connell and Howard make some agreement with their eyes, count out loud 1-2-3 (*Why are they counting?*) as I'm crawling past and with Colt pistols shoot each other. God blind me, scares the hell out of me. Two shots and two heads half-destroyed. Couldn't the double-cunted arseholes shoot a few more dog soldiers before leaving the rest of us short of good men?

Arrows fly up in awful flocks. You do not know what arrows are like pulled back by strong men, by devils, and drawn in by us *wasichu*. A good bow can drill an arrow through rock or an army wagon. A storm lifts with its weird whizzing sound and drifts down in our legs and backs, pinning us to yellow prairie, snowflake horses and red speckled horses stepping through slim chokecherry shafts. Hundreds of arrows rattle and hum and I can't even see who is shooting them.

We were touching heels but finally no one else is left alive but Jackie Lyons and his fecking arrow in his spine and me using someone else's Lancaster rifle behind someone else's horse-flesh, in yellow land by a liver chestnut horse that could have been good, silver river looping below like an earring, wrinkled bluffs above my eyes.

We've got 'em boys, the blond ass said when first on the high ridge. We came here looking for trouble.

Jackie with his arrowhead is still screaming for Doctor Jesu and I tell him to be of good cheer and then I run away from yellow-eyed Jackie and the others, bolt like a coward from the bleeding bodies of my companions, run low toward a ravine that is already a graveyard for Smith's E Company.

My bootsteps seem so loud, everything noisy and slow, sliding into willow thickets and wild roses. My skin torn, lightning flashing up my elbow where it hits rock. Maybe I can hide in river thickets until dark, find the drunkard Reno's men.

An Indian in a sailor's monkey jacket and a red woollen shirt dances, lifting a long sabre, but it cannot be one of ours; we left our sabres packed in wooden boxes at Powder River.

Indians in bear coats wave shiny government axes they were given as gifts at some peace parley. Thoughtful of the politicians to arm both sides in the fracas.

On the slope I see women using axes and knives and stone hammers on our fallen soldiers, see the women pull off the young soldiers' pants and slice at what is between their legs. Some men, pretending to be dead, jump up at that news, at that knife nudging their nethers. Some men jump up and the women and boys fall away from them, terrified of spirits back from the place. Some men jump up, then are hammered back down into the new world, the spirit world. No longer pretending. Shots ring out, hoarse voices call names. John! *John! Oh mother!* We fly and we crawl and we bleed. Horses flattened and gloves and hats and carbines around bloody pale bodies. It is June, summer in Montana Territory. I don't know how Major Reno is doing, where he is, how many of us are left.

I delve deeper into the draw's modest scrub willow, clamber on hands and knees in the red branches, shifting my hiding spot; young boys fire arrows into my thicket and the young devils laugh when I am hit in the calf and can not help but yelp. Blood running in my hair and blood dripping from my leg and I am going to be killed by children with shining eyes. They find me amusing. They can not see me but I lack dignity, an adult crawling back and forth like a clumsy blue lizard.

Children with smallpox scars laugh at me and try to murder me as boys will with a frog or a snake in a bush, as I used to do with my cousins along the Red River, as the Orangemen did with poor Goulet.

I am panicking as I crawl about on hands and knees like a cur, not staying long in one spot, arrows and rocks crashing knobby branches. They toy with me, their laughter ringing my small refuge, and I am primed to give up hiding and run again when a green recruit from E Company, naked and bleeding from eyes and crotch, staggers past. He escaped the women with stone hammers but now my young boys chase after him with a whoop and a holler. Dripping with blood he looks so richly white, as if bleached by the diseased laundry girls that follow the 7th. We are rich in princes. A new victim is always more intriguing than the familiar victim. The poor bleeding recruit saves me for a few seconds.

I fall down in a flowered rocky draw, banging both knee-pans; crawl right into the rock, into a long crack that might protect me from the flint and gold arrowheads. Pushing willow back, I lie in the crevasse and let the ugly bush bounce back to cover my grave, and I shove flat pieces of sandstone and fistfuls of dust over my feet and legs and chest until only my French nose stands up to betray me. I am dead in the ground. My knees and elbow and head throb and the whole glinting river valley lit by low billows of dust and smoke. In the sky several suns drift; sundogs swim around them. I knew we should have stayed away from this country.

Riders with bloody masks and wolf voices and stolen blue uniforms sweep one way and others sweep back down until they hit a high riverbank or a coulee or a ridge and turn again, riders perched lightly on their mustangs as if playing on a pia-no stool. One horse drags the remains of some recruit. See what the ground does to you, the smallest bump or boulder. When that boy of ours falls to pieces the noble savages tie up another boy for their amusement and then that young boy falls to pieces on the bloody end of the hemp while his mother sits talking to a parson in a parlour in Ohio. This I watch from my grave of slatey stone and wildflowers, watch my friends torn apart, seeing too much, an underground man, knee high to a June bug, limp as a neck-wrung rooster.

Horses with red hands and suns painted on their flanks stumble over bodies or shy away with crazy eyes as the 7th Cavalry's paper money blows around, hundreds of bloodied dollars decorating our bone orchard. The Indians like silver, don't know paper money. Christ's foot I am thirsty and would give any amount of that bloody money for a cup of river-water or malt beer or even bluestone gin. We were paid day before the march, paid in the middle of nowhere so we couldn't run off. All this money useless to us here, useless to dead men. If I get out of here I'll hang onto a dollar, I'll squeeze it until that eagle grins. Or I'll spend it fast as I can, go on a jag of ribsteak and blue potatoes and growlers of Leinenkugel's ale every damn day and night till I die of a knife and fork, put down my knife and fork and big clay mug and lie on goosedown. Christ on a crutch I am thirsty. I slip grass and pebbles into my mouth. Thirsty! Past sweat, my throat made of timber. I don't want a knife to my privates. I want a tumble down the sink. Why on earth do people want to cut up other people? I have seen too much of it on both sides. Why do the women like it so? I believe some of these Indian women would skin a flea for hide and tallow.

Our brevet general lived for a long time with a very young Indian woman, was sharing blanket duty with his brother Tom. I don't know if his wife Elizabeth knew; she may have. Lo the Indian, say the popular verses. Many of us, including Iron Butt himself, had to get the mercury treatment for the clap. Calamity Jane followed us wearing lice and the clothes of a man. Our deadbeat outfit was often drunk as lords, drunk as a boiled owl, trading coffin-varnish whiskey to the Sioux for buffalo tongues and onions, or *grosse bosse,* the big hump those animals ferry for us like camels, or tender *dépouilles,* that tasty soft flesh under the ribs.

From inside my grave I watch as men I'd drank pine-top barleycorn with and ate bison tongue with and marched with wearing creased American boots have their private skulls broken into, like a head is a Chinese box, and their tongues and live brains pulled out and set up on rocks in some kind of display. Howdy James, Hello Will. The boys' arms are broken, feet cut right off, teeth chopped out with axes, and eyes turned into tiny tomatoes placed carefully on whited ledges. Our daubed and greased enemies don't want us to see or dance in the afterlife. I see Adam's apples cut from men's throats. They don't want us to have throats in the next world; no more crackers and whiskey, songs and cursing. No Latin prayers or laughing drabble-tail whores. They want us to have nothing there in the afterlife, not a thing, not even a voice singing ballads about Garry Owen or a brain recalling the Panic of '73 that pushed me here in '76.

All those boyos who deserted over the months, got sick of

army life and took the Grand Bounce, took French Leave, gone hunting for Montana Territory gold or hiring with the railroad or shooting buffalo for 400 a hide, Wellsir now I think them smart for clearing out, avoiding this, although many of those deserters may be long dead in other spectral greedy ambushes, boots yanked off their corpses and cut into pieces for the soft sweaty leather.

I think of my cousins up in Pembina and Batoche and St. Laurent and Duck Lake, running a flat-bottom ferry *(Best Scow on the River* says the poster on a poplar) and hunting and farming strips of land to the mahogany river's edge. A peaceful cabin with a lantern glowing yellow and blue in a parchment window. Batoche is not that far north of where I hide in this ravine. In a week or two I could walk there, call out from the yard. Remember me? The one who left? Show them my wounds.

I wait some time and the warriors seem to shift south to a copse of timber above the river, perhaps pulled to Reno's men or Benteen or to flummox themselves, and when they're gone a bit I rise from my grave and crawl north to where I started, where my dead horse lies, where I lost track of time, of early light and late light.

Jackie Lyons has dozens of arrows in him now The arrow is gone from the hole in my calf though I don't remember pulling it. The Indians set up Jackie on his hands and knees and then shot arrows at his back end for sport. By running like a coward I missed that.

Pieces of bodies at my feet. Three heads cut off and

arranged in a circle, staring sternly past each other, as if just finished arguing. Three heads and I know them. One bearded head used to play hornpipes on a cracked fiddle and you think, Johnny Reb, the ex-Confederate Irish Volunteer, why is your head bleeding red and black pitch on the dusty prairie? Laughing boys come to kill. Can I patch you boyos back together? You salty pilgrims squeezed through so many skirmishes and lung wounds and border wars, then Custer forced us in here. The bugle sounded for a while on this hill and then it stopped.

George Armstrong Custer is wounded but still alive just north of the three severed heads, Iron Butt Custer with blood coming out of his girlish mouth, Custer still alive with four dead officers sitting in a circle around him as if having China tea, and not with their men, their own companies. Why aren't they with their men? It is a strange scene, swallowtailed silk guidons fallen on the ground, the blond devil alive, and the dead circle of sycophants still trying to listen to him under clouds like ripped stunsails and golden light on the river and treed islands below.

When we first snuck in here I saw an Indian man peacefully washing a horse in the river — that seems so long ago.

Custer is shot in the side, just one wound that I can see. Custer's eyes are intense, one side in shadow, and he seems to be thinking hard, looking around but seeing God knows what. This vain man, famous for a handsome countenance, now looks like he'd been weaned on a pickle.

My skin is darker and coloured with blood and earth, nay

hair black, and I'm out of uniform, half-naked, a grimy wild-man, but Custer calls as if we're old friends, as if we often shared lemonade and ginger-cakes in his tent with the cast iron stove that was so heavy to haul about.

Trooper, he says to me, waving his pistol. We've driven them off. Custer, at this moment, strikes me as someone who gets out of bed to turn over so his blankets last longer.

Custer cut his hair short before we left Dakota Territory and wrecked our luck, but *his* damn luck has held. He's had yet another horse shot out from underneath him but he's survived. Bodies bristling with arrows but not his body. Others have their entrails slip out and their entrails tied up with other men's entrails but Custer's white skin is almost pristine. Custer's famous luck.

I pick up his hat from the dust and skewed legs of the dead officers. I'm going to keep the brevet general's hat.

Tom, Custer calls. Tom, are you there? Boston? We must get back to Elizabeth. Autie, are you holding on? Where are my greyhounds?

He is alive and mad in all this carnage. George Armstrong Iron Butt Custer looks very old. It's almost supper, I'd guess, and I'm very hungry and my eyes are sore. I need to take care of a small detail. He's still waving his pistol.

I move my hand slowly. With his own pistol and squeezing his own finger on the trigger I shoot George Custer in the temple and George Custer topples against one of the four men lying around him like a crib, smiling as he leaves a world. He looks happier. I expect more gore after what I have seen on this hellish hillside but the tiny hole in his balding blonde head hardly shows. I assume there is more of a mess just inside that private place, inside his version. of the Chinese box puzzle.

I help George Custer shoot George Custer and begin a long trip with a step, another step, limping north wrapped in lice, wrapped in a dead Indian's twenty-dollar blanket and wearing Custer's floppy hat, my bloody head where his bloody head was.

I dodge down into the next dip after our gory ridge, and what do I spy but a murder of crows and a spooked U.S. 7th mare with the reins dragging and a picket stake bouncing behind on a hemp rope. Close by in the grass is a dead soldier with a hole in his face and his pistol lying by him and crows looking him over. I believe the crazy cuss got free of the aborigines, but shot himself, expecting a wave of them over the smoky ridge, believing himself doomed surely.

I pick up the suicide's pistol, catch his spooked horse, and coax it toward Rupert's Land, toward Canada, coax my wrecked knee-pans, sky going crimson and yellow over the benchlands. I have some hardtack. I lost all my sugar and coffee and bacon back there, my letters and my crackers and molasses. I used to have anything I wanted when I was younger, anything, and it meant nothing at the time.

Nights I hobble the horse, trying to sleep before the hard-mouthed mare gets too far away, riding and walking on my sore legs, my bashed knees, the two of us fording or swimming the Yellowstone and the Redwater and the Missouri and Poplar Creek, drinking from a river and waiting for the next stream or lake to drink, crossing squatting hills of creeping purple lizards and red rattlesnakes and roses and berries that haven't ripened yet, watching redtail hawks and buffalo wolves and the poisoned carcasses, walking the suicide's tired horse toward Montagne de Cypres and Batoche and peace with my uncle and Dufresne and Father André. Keeping grassfire smoke to the south of me, pushing north, sun burning me badly despite Custer's hat.

Beside a small creek I drink and then attempt sign language with three Indians in the skins of beasts who talk of the crazy whites shooting each other or cowards who threw their weapons away weeping, and I think of my rifle jamming and I want to weep and curse again. They all know within hours what has happened, pluck the news from the air. Their scalp-locks stick up. Like a dream they surprised me at the stream. Are they Crow? Cree? I hope so. The stream likely has no name. The three men examine me and my horse with suspicion, mumble about my suicide's pistol and my knife, an old Arkansas toothpick. My blanket is full of lice. My skin is burnt black, blisters and pustules rising on my nose, my lips swollen. I listen to them and keep my burnt mouth closed.

Sioux did not kill Custer, I want to say. Lakota, no. Cheyenne did not kill Custer. Rain in the Face did not kill Custer. White Bull or Wooden Leg did not kill Custer. Hump did not kill Custer. Crazy Horse or Spotted Eagle did not kill Custer. Tantanka Yatanka and the Dreamers did not kill Custer. I killed Iron Butt. I want to steal it from them, own it like a seized pocket-watch.

I have Irish blood, Scottish blood, Cree blood, and French

blood. I wish to keep that mixed blood safe inside me, keep it apart from the dust of this destroyed summer where grasshoppers replace buffalo.

I still have my hands and feet. No one has chopped them off. No one has hammered my teeth out with a rock or set up my brain or eyes on a rock table.

Iskotawapoo, they wonder: fire liquid, blind tiger. No, I insist, No, for these three will kill me if they think I'm a whiskey trader and I'm alone. I could use a drink of blind tiger. I don't want my face to betray that the suicide's pistol has no bullets left. If it enters my mind it may enter their mind.

If I can get back over the border, I'll settle down near Batoche, a gentleman farmer playing a cracked fiddle like Johnny Reb. Wolfskins stretched and lantern glowing yellow and blue in a tiny window and no more stone hammers to the brains, no more Orangeman horsewhips or bayonets at my backside. No more hacking and reeking trouble. I am from north of Assiniboine and I can keep my mouth shut, not like some of these Texans in the 7th.

The lice in my blanket trouble me. I see an anthill. I stir the anthill with a willow branch, churning deep, irritating them, and then I lay my blanket down on the dirt as the three watch my naked back. Frenzied red ants, streaming out to defend their ruined home, pick the lice clean from my borrowed blanket.

They'll leave us be in Batoche. Isidore and Jean and all my uncles and aunts and cousins dancing in my poplar cabin so snug you can't curse the dog without getting fur in your teeth.

Railroads gone broke and ants picking off lice and these three with greased scalp-locks looking at my naked back and wondering whether to kill me or let me cross.

19 Knives

he's pleased to meet you underneath the horse
—Elliott Smith, *Speed Trials*

Carol my caseworker vouched that I was reliable enough for carry privileges, so they let me have a week's worth of methadone to take home, instead of driving every day to the pharmacy across the island, especially since I had my boy to take care of. Carol knew I wouldn't sell the meth, knew those days were over.

Back in the days — way back — my buddies were salmon fishermen, buckets of money, growing on trees back then working mildew fishboats way up the rainy green coast. Lost cedar inlets with hot springs and bleached totem poles. Too much cash flying like loose leaves through marina bars and government wharves, and the fish piled in dead heaps in the mist, in icy holds and bilgewater that smelled of money and diesel.

No needles at first. We only snorted heroin, a sport and a pastime, the conventional wisdom being that it's not addictive when just snorting I planned to stop after a few lost weekends and get back to normal, but something failed me, old school words gave up the ghost, crackers in soup, and new vague words clouded through me like trained white mice.

Those Vietnamese boys in Nanaimo had that good pure stuff, stepped on with a little lidocaine to keep you lining up for more.

Just a taste, I insisted, that's all.

Those skinny Viet boys almost giving it away, points of China white going for ten or twenty bucks, deliver it by discreet courier, so the train kept arolling, and then a year or two later you're boiling up ammonia on the stovetop and the car has an expired temporary permit in the back window and your Swiss cheese brain is pawning your father's sax and you've spent enough to buy a space station.

Here's the funny thing: I always *despised* junkies, shunned their inhabited hectic arms, sleepy syllables, and sybarite synapses. Look at those bozos, I said, can't see a hole in a ladder. I thought I was smarter than the rest with my hornet-hive head. My earthly powers I believed to be manifold, special, hard as teeth on a chainsaw. I knew I could handle it, *knew.*

I mix my meth with the sweetest orange juice I can find, because the meth is so bitter. It's really gross. A strip of masking tape on my juice, where I wrote in big felt pen: DO NOT DRINK!! I knew my boy loved OJ. I put it in the door away from the regular milk and juice and Kool-Aid containers.

I said, "The stuff in the door is my special medicine." I said, "Don't — touch — anything — in — the — door." I made it very clear. I could not have made it clearer.

My boy is a light sleeper. My boy wakes up in the middle of the night, our little house quiet. My boy loves orange juice, would say, "I need a dur-rink, Dad." He wakes up thirsty, a thirst like me, a night owl like me, like me his glasses folded on his nightstand, the night sky violet, quiet as a pyramid in the desert, no one up in our little house, kitchen clock ticking like an IV drip.

Maybe he's half asleep, floor cool, floating in pale pyjamas, ghostly, across our kitchen floor to the fridge, hesitates like a blank tape.

I couldn't inject myself at first. I needed help. Others helped, they fixed me, my costive pals summoned it up. Like a good Catholic I grew to love the ritual, admire the finely engineered syringe poised above like a needlenosed hummingbird waiting for you, so precisely tooled, the tiny opening rent, opening.

The door open, fridge light on the lino like blue light by the sea. The salmon are gone now and the boats are quiet and chained to the dock, and Carol and the College of Physicians knew I was okay to take a week's worth home.

The Nazis developed methadone in World War II; but they called it Adolphine, thought it sweet enough to name it after Adolph. Up to eighty mil a day. It's not the real thing. I tried to join the Pepsi generation but they said I failed the physical. Outside in my yard is a pileated woodpecker, a baby. I don't know if it's going to make it through the night. Now I hear things at night, or when I'm down in the crawl space, hear my boy walking the floor to the white fridge: this is my new addiction, my crown of thorns, my Jones I can't kick. Like him, I wake up and need a drink.

Once I bought my boy a hot dog at the zoo and he dropped the hot dog on the ground and I hit him in the stomach and said, "What the hell are you doing?!" and now I wish I could tell him that it's okay to drop his hot dog, that there are worse things I know of now. I wish I could say to him admirable things, buy him that booster pack of Japanese Pokémon cards that he was always asking after or that full-colour book on Egyptian mummies, or take a spin at Island Go-Karts.

Start out chippying, but later you need three bags just to be barely all right. You just keep shooting it in, you give and you give, many hoofprints going in but none coming out. You think of the boy's blond mother, a singer from Montana. She moves through the fair, moves through the airport with balloons of it hidden in her stomach, praying they don't burst.

I was waiting for her in the bar. Tight as the bark on a tree, I was waiting and waiting (but she didn't make it) at the ersatz-

Tudor pub by the piers. The inside decor was Mexican — an uneasy Tudor-Mexican alliance.

"The code is so brutal I can barely edit it," some tech said to a vibrating table of drinks.

Exactly, I thought. No more stuttering white thrill, no golden robot vibe, no leaping the garden wall. Instead you just want to *not* feel sick. That's what your meeting with God turns into. And you want to change before it's too late, want to change your outfit.

After he drank my orange juice he wouldn't wake up in his bed, open those eyelids, no longer a light sleeper. Meth is a slow-acting narcotic, shuts down the respiratory. I knew the symptoms. I called an ambulance to carry him to the hospital.

I knew the hospital because three years ago a policeman shot me in someone else's backyard. The intruder, locks on your backdoor, the tangled squares of night. One moment standing, next a flash, and it felt like a wheelbarrow hit me, knocked me down, but my hat staying on my head the whole time. I flipped to the ground in the rich careful houses (I found my boy crumpled), the sky on mute, hat still on my head.

The policeman claimed I pulled a knife, so he shot me. I had no knife.

An ambulance came to visit my lamentations. The paramedics with their equipment ran bent over as if there were chopper blades cutting above us. I wanted to be witty, make a good impression, didn't want to be on someone's patio crying.

The police sealed off the yard so they could look for the knife in daylight. They needed that important evidence.

Next morning nineteen knives lay in the grass of that small yard. Every cop in town must have driven by and flipped a knife over the fence.

I don't blame them for taking care of their own. I should have taken better care of my own. His sleepy eyes, spotting my OJ in the fridge door, forbidden fruit, my small boy in Pjs, peering around with a ghost of a smile. We decide things lightly, pursue our pleasures.

At first the paramedics tried the kiss of life, tried driving in a needle of Narcan. How fine he looked in his pale pyjamas. His eyelids. The driver drove and I rode in the back of the familiar ambulance, thinking of that Neil Young line: *An ambulance can only go so fast.*

We got to the hospital but it was no good. Locks on the door but I brought the intruder into our little two bedroom bungalow. We decide things.

At first I just snorted. Nothing serious. A little pick me up, like ten-cent suicide wings, the good kind, dry as kindling. Now I hear him walking.

My boy was smart, loved yacking while I drove him around logging roads. He took first place in spelling bees at school, was fascinated by his library books on ancient Egyptians and their mummies and pyramids, their journeys to the underworld.

The embalmers pulled out internal organs but kept them in beautiful containers with lid handles the likeness of the pharaoh's head.

We drove around together, and I had a decent car. We were putting my life back together.

Egyptians washed the dead body with oil and spices, but they didn't keep the brain, didn't seem to value the brain. Why is that, he wondered.

We were driving in the Electra, flathatting it to a lake up in the clouds. My boy was in the backseat so he had room to play and read. He didn't get carsick reading there. From the backseat he told me all about the Egyptians preparing the body for safe passage to the afterlife, how the spirit was in two worlds — one world during the day, but at night, travelling back to the body. They worked over the body, made it hollow. With a long hook, they removed the brain through the nose.

Swinger

. . . devise engines for my life.
—Iago

The night bus drops me on Telegraph Bay Road and I walk in on the dark lane high above the sea's scored granite. My black leather jacket gives one message; my clean white tennis shoes convey another: these shoes attempt to show I'm actually okay.

This winding lane in the firs has no lights and there is no moon tonight. I walk on the left side, almost in the trees, my gait unsteady on the uneven grass verge. Owls call high in the swaying Douglas firs, and I think of those two barmy English-men hooting in their little back gardens every night, two men making ersatz owl noises, thinking the other person a real owl answering them. This goes on for years, then they find they are twins, there are no screech owls, no great horned owls in their gardens. There are two men in anoraks calling to each other in the suburbs. Their story is in all the newspapers.

In the dark night, with flesh and blood owls, I walk, thinking, Why tell the press? Wouldn't you keep quiet? Wouldn't you feel like a right *twit?*

Then the police van, a blinding light, and I can't see the man talking from behind the light. It's irritating. The disembodied voice asks what I'm doing here, where I'm going.

Home.

Where is home? the voice in the light asks.

I say to the voice, Either explain the problem or let me go home.

I'm in a bit of a foul mood, the exact wrong mood for this — cuts at work, problems at home, no patience with the kids, never enough sleep.

Okay wise guy, he says, coming toward me.

I'm not going to put up with this crap, I think.

Push comes to shove, swinging each other round and round, then the other man hits the van's side mirror, hits the mirror hard with his head, those big west coast mirrors, and he drops like he's been clotheslined, this counsellor now most still, most grave, one of those with a glass jaw.

The van running, time stopped, huge light still glaring on our pale limbs; arclight on fused blue leaves, and a white plastic bag in the ditch seems a comment, a witness. When I get a chance to look at him, I'm not sure he's actually a policeman: generic white shirt and black pants and shoes. Is he working plainclothes? I don't know. To me he looks relieved.

Inside the van I find an old soft green cushion, a *Dukes of Hazzard* lunchbox. Inside is a cookie, a big glittering M&M cookie. I put the green cushion under his head, drape his jacket over him like a blanket, and leave his lunchbox on the road beside him. The police radio says calm things, numerals and words from a bored female dispatcher. I eat his big cookie.

I take the van home, park it on the dark lawn past the carport so the car can get out in the morning. We're way up a long driveway in the fir trees — no one can see us, it'll be okay. I'll have to ditch the van sometime soon, but I'm too lazy just this instant.

In the morning my wife is gone for the earlybird swim. Maybe she's never coming back, maybe she has left town and my car is abandoned at the cornfield airport or ghostly grey Greyhound depot. I have to take my boy to kindergarten! What on earth is this world coming to?! My boy and I migrate fitfully around the ugly carport slab.

Daddy has a police van!!

My boy is excited. I have to confess I kind of like that.

Yes, Daddy *does* have a police van.

My boy asks, Does this van go *top speed!?*

Well now son, let's just see about that.

We go very fast until we see two little old ladies from the neighbourhood, and we slow out of respect.

Girls you looking mighty fine! I bugle over the police van's loudspeaker and the ladies giggle, pleased, putting their little old lady hands to their little old lady mouths.

I think, Maybe I could keep the van just for a while.

I wear clean white shirts, clean blue shirts, wear Vietnam era aviator shades. I look okay piloting this van.

At first I just drive the one road to school, then other roads, expand my range. No one stops me. The van starts to feel like mine. Yes. Daddy has a police van, patrolling headlands and bluffs, the school, the playground, the white church that looks like an alien craft crashing at an angle.

I start watching people, a collector.

Skateboarders: *Get off your board!* My sudden voice bellowing on the intimate inhuman speaker.

Firecrackers and rockets: *Stop that right now.*

Taggers spray the bus shelter by Telegraph Bay Road: *Hey you!*

Whassup fool?

Move it along, I suggest.

That's fucked up.

I aim a little pepper spray his way.

That's even more fucked up, he says, tears streaming. Eeek, he says, bent over.

You said a mouthful, *dude,* I utter.

I hate this gloomy time of year, he weeps, eyes on fire, eyes oniony globes.

We in the business refer to pepper spray as *manners in a can.*

A redhaired kid with a pipe bomb on the suburban mountain; the bomb takes his hand off just as he throws it at my van. I cannot stop him. His loyal friends run and leave him sobbing on the flat stone of the mountaintop and I pick him up bodily and drop him at the small hospice nuns have hidden in the pines past the wrecked ice plant with its walls going to sponge under winter rains and wandering stars.

For reasons unclear to me, while in my van, I run into people in crisis mode, when they are in hot tears and spasmodics.

My father wound his watch at the same time every day, believed the watch machinery was happier with routine. After the war he seemed to find a life that avoided hot tears and spasmodics. He had a metal watchband cut from a crashed Battle of Britain Spitfire Supermarine. When he died he had a newer watch on. The coroner gave it to me in an envelope. Where did that silver piece of Spitfire fly away to?

Fall. Carnival tents blossoming on the edge of town, the flats by the bay, the last dusty road, the calliope and giraffe and panther in the lurking trees, suspicious hermaphrodites, suspicious characters all, I assume, but I have a quick nightcap with Lizardboy and Woman Who Didn't Finish Her Degree and the Author Who Is Happy With His Agent — these performers (I avoid judging them as freaks) seem okay, they seem really down to earth.

We talk and drink outside the tiny trailers housing other strange and wonderful circus attractions: a collection of strange wondrous rarities, but just like you and me in some ways. They put on their pants one leg at a time. The Carnival of the Newly Blind puts on a damn good show, and they hand me comp tickets for the whole family, which is mighty white of them.

A drink tomorrow night? Certainly.

I will slip back to the floodplain with black flowers and blush wine, to sleep with the carnival girl in the serious van, howler monkeys roaming their trees, our brains roaring their tangled trees.

When I touch her skin tomorrow night, it will be like fingers on a familiar scar. As we ease toward some distant revelation, toward some red furnace star, she will whisper to my ear (and I am all ears), she will whisper while breathing, Think of me (pause) as the concept (pause) made flesh (pause) and made blood Think of me as *Infotainment* become manifest in greasepaint and panties. Yes sir, we will both exclaim at the same time.

Her hand on me I think of as my due. A red apple from a grocer.

Leave in the van and the performers climb to their spots behind the shadowed glass.

O to fill up with unleaded under yon leafy yew tree, to purchase chocolate coffee at the deli, to roll through hailstones past Our Aghast Lady of the Tumour.

I take care of my neighbourhood, my weighted territory — pulling over big boats ploughing through slush, fenders acned with Bondo. I keep an eye on things. I take care of things. I see young couples kissing in their puffy parkas. I don't see my wife or boy much anymore. It's not easy, it gets to you. Perceiving the world with different eyes. But I drive the van. I keep going.

A quiet weeknight — no moon — going home in my van

with its black and white plumage. I spy a male walking alone, dark jacket, sneakers, left side of our road high above the granite sea. He looks suspicious. Just a hunch.

Where you going? I ask reasonably.

What's the problemo? he sputters. Why aren't you out catching the real criminals?

Easy, scout, just want to know ...

Know? Know! What about I know my rights!

Oh, another jailhouse lawyer wants to break my balls. Let's just see what material this buttinski joker's made of, I decide.

I put on the blinding white light, define our stage, my rage, rest of the world receded, guilt there like a naked bulb.

I climb out of the van with my cadence and pepper spray, my *manners in a can, and* I go to settle his law school hash, but he grabs me close, pulls me to his body like a single-minded lover. Two of us shove and pull, swing each other swiftly, blurred jackets and canvas shoes dancing on ivory gravel, round and round the verge, faster and faster like calliope music and falling arbutus branches, blurring sleeves and white mirror, jittery coastline spinning like a carnival merry-go-round, the stone headland and seals in the gnashing breakers with their old man heads. Our black monkey world made tiny in bleach smoking light, and the mystery woman on the police radio sounds concerned about #18.

We swing, really flying, and I think of two male brains, two harmless parties in darkest Britain out behind a fenced semi-detached, throwing double fake owl calls, wanting to connect with mystery and hooked beaks and predators, predators, waiting to connect with a wild world that is pointedly not England's polite backyard or crowded tube escalators *(Mind the gap),* wanting to light out for tender tenantless territories, and *#18? Are you there? Do you copy?*

Uranium City Rollers

The impulse to cruelty is almost as violent as
the impulse to sexual love.
— A. Huxley

God sends meat and the devil sends cooks.
—Thomas Delony, *c. 1550-1600*

Birds topping the rise bathed in talented light, floating our flowered town, and darkest sea downhill mint-
ing foggy sunshine. On this outdoor deck we ride tables of
black lager, remembering winter storms — log-booms tear-
ing themselves apart in oiled surf, pale breakers pulling rivets from a boat, and clawing bones and wrinkled bodies and
tiny Chinese skulls from the seaside graveyard — but now
the sun warms us, and we imbibe fragrant malts, narcolep-
tic grains, skunky hops; we ride the turpentine pine hill by
the female arts college, refresh each other on the non-issues.

Heads and haircuts turn to an angry woman's voice. This woman, this voice, cuts harder and deeper than the clean younger clientele. Most of us are pushed out of the same machine, agreeing on intonation, information, tongues, tenor, teeth. Our families like to think we're above hewing wood, carrying water, though we will stoop to burn data on the cube farm and we will pearl-dive at the Hard Rock Cafe on Banff Avenue.

This scoured voice begs to differ, has been around the block a few times.

"Why are you telling Zeke this? Are you trying to embarrass me? Why are you doing this? I'll end our business relationship right now!"

The angry woman's hair is short, a dark brown Prince Valiant cut. The angry woman is wearing a blue sweatshirt with a picture of a canoe sailing across a lake, a canoe sailing across her big chest. Canoe Woman is shouting at a drunken man with a watermelon mound of a stomach, a confused man in brown polyester pants.

Drunk Polyester Guy stammers, "I'm not trying to embarrass ..."

Canoe Woman says, "Don't fuck with me."

"... anyone ..."

This couple in their forties sticks out. Drunk Polyester Guy has a big face ridged like a homemade pie. Two men sitting with the couple look tense, plotters seeing something simple go awry. These two I know a little — Zeke and Fergus. Zeke and

Fergus are older than the fresh-faced lounge crowd but younger than the arguing couple.

"Jeez, you're getting paranoid in your old age," Drunk Polyester Guy mutters, trying to chuckle, joke with the guys and isolate her. His strategy seems a mistake. He's not taking Canoe Woman seriously, plus he insults her (*your old age*).

"I am not *paranoid,*" Canoe Woman says tersely, avoiding the age issue.

"You are."

"Am not."

"Are so."

They bicker like children, jab like pecking chickens; we decide they have known each other a long time. She's had assertiveness training, is not letting him off the hook.

"Why are you telling this story? What is the point?!"

"Yes well, okay, I agree, that's fine, I didn't even bring it up." He's trying to backtrack now.

"Zeke knows about me now," she says in a sad voice. "He doesn't know."

Zeke sits saying nothing, shades over his eyes. Zeke has a small impassive face, thinning hair, a thick walrus mustache, a briefcase. No one else has shades. Zeke knows now

"Zeke's okay," Drunk Polyester Guy says.

She says, "I was going through a really really hard time then when that . .

"Well so was I," he counters, slurring.

"I'm not proud of — no, I *am* proud," she decides.

"Well, maybe I might have embarrassed you. But listen. Listen. This is the thing, that night, I won a hundred bucks, serious money, and I met this chick, a gorgeous chick, red dress cut down to here, a red dress! Chick says, Well sport, care to pinch these babies, think you can run with these puppies? Well sure but just my luck the bouncer decides ..."

Fergus rises from the plastic table without a word. Fergus has a blond buzzcut, acne scars, silver glasses, is ex-navy, ugly and slouchy. He has lasted a decade in student politics, although there is some Student Union money scandal in his past, tavern funds disappearing, perhaps a connection to slothful edgy pharmaceuticals . Like me, he can never leave school because his loans are too high. We sign up for more and more obscure courses, and will soon know everything. I know a little about him, can tell they're working some angle with this couple.

"Where ya going, bud?"

Fergus says nothing in reply. Fergus walks away.

"He's bored of you," says Canoe Woman. "Your little stories."

"Where, wha?"

She sits up, a brainstorm hitting, "You know, I think you're *jealous* of how things are going for me."

Canoe Woman likes this idea. Her voice relaxes, she stops arguing.

Canoe Woman says, "I'm on a *happy thing* now and nothing's going to bring Inc down — not you or your stupid stories. I'm on a happy thing now"

Curious wasps do recon on our glass rims, the first wasps of spring. Three students have finished exams and are celebrating; other students haven't finished exams but are getting faced anyway, out of respect, out of professional courtesy.

She says, "You know, I've been dealing a long time. I've got juice with certain parties. Two years is a *long* time. There it is. They know me now"

"You ever take Shakespeare, Zeke?"

"Everyone does Shakespeare. There's a law"

"Think they spoke like that day to day, that iambic diameter, that Look at yon russet sun rising on yon mildew loaf of bread?"

Zeke doesn't answer from behind his walrus mustache and tinted lenses. Drunken Polyester Guy drinks and considers Shakespeare. "Willie the Shake never played Nintendo," he says.

"This one owes me money," Canoe Woman says. "Drinking my beer. This one owes me, Mr. Plumber to the Stars."

"Oh and you're such a winner," Drunk Polyester Guy says.

"I am. You're *jealous.*"

"See what I have to put up with?" he says. He's still trying to joke. He has no idea what they want to hear. "She's very aggressive that way. Oh oh, I forgot to put some change under my kid's pillow. Darn darn darn!"

Male and female mallards whistle overhead in admirable formation. In World War II this plateau by the sea was an RCAF training field. Farmboys levitated from here to dogfight in cheesecloth Hawker Hurricanes, to battle Wilhelm Messerschmitt's sublime creations, to sink the *Tirpitz* in a Norwegian fjord with 12,000-pound Tallboy bombs through the ship's armoured deck. Farmboys went from here to aero-dromes named Skipton-on-Swale and Goosepool Tees-side, were shot down in screaming flak and black smoke and ack-ack over Rotterdam or Dresden while dribbling incendiary bombs from the belly of a Lancaster X or a Halifax heavy bomber.

Now we fly here in 747s to wear nose rings and corporate ballcaps. We come to spend our parents' money on corporate beer and nachos. On the chalkboard menu Ray spells this *na-tcho's just* to bug me and the handful of post-doc people. Ray the bartender calls out, "32! Large nachos with!" Ray calls out, "33, your fingers are up!" Ray the bartender pours us doubles and plays shiny CDs. We eat fake Tex-Mex, listen to fake Celt-ic, listen to a rock band try to be about rebellion and fail to be about rebellion. Fast black crows drop out of clean white cu-mulus sheets, rabbits and grackles move nervously in the crack-ling bush, and I decide drinking in shorts is fundamentally different than drinking in long pants.

"Split a deck?" Zeke wonders. Canoe Woman plunges in-side to buy smokes.

Drunk Polyester Guy says, "Zeke, that story about *her* — that story about her she doesn't want me to tell, she stopped me — well that story could've got *real juicy.*"

"Yeah yeah," Zeke mumbles. He too walks inside in his short seventies leather jacket. He has silver keys jangling on the hip of his jeans. Zeke is thin, legs like cigarettes.

"Real juicy story," says Drunk Polyester Guy to no one. *404, we think, no document there.*

Eventually Drunk Polyester Guy shuffles inside, follows Fergus and Zeke and Canoe Woman. Inside I hear sounds of smashing glass and yelling. Out on the deck I can't tell who's smashing glass, if the glass detonating is deliberate or accidental, I lack information, don't know if Drunk Polyester Guy's having his big pie *face* sliced open. Who ordered a shrimp salad? wonders the PA.

Drunk Polyester Guy comes back to the table alone, his pie face sad but unbloodied, his posture sad, his motions aimless as a janitor's broom. He pulls on his houndstooth sportscoat. Has Ray eighty-sixed him? Was there a brawl? An accident? Is he cast out of our lovely garden of grackles and rabbits and wild roses bobbing in the sea breeze?

He reminds me of a friend I made years back in Uranium City. Drunk Polyester Guy wears a white dress shirt but his stomach dislodges the dress shirt, destroys the effect. He has attempted to match his brown polyester pants with a natty sportscoat, but transports with him the dazed aura of an unmade bed, a creature constantly rising from tangling airless sheets.

His big face amiable and puzzled, a fat neck: too many years of beer falling down that throat, layers to that throat like rings on a tree, his heart pumping hard with pepper and gravy and Fig Newtons and nacho cheese. I hadn't thought about Uranium City in a long time: far to the north of where I am now, men working the face deep in radioactive tunnels, burly men with mine rash moving ore and throwing away their money in the bar. We had a hot little band in Uranium City, played the Alkaloid Hotel tavern, had lives and bottles and nubby hotel bedspreads, a stand-up bass, parlayed slide guitar with a knife and a fuzzy Dressler tube amp, played wanton acid Motown: "Walking the Dog," "Wine Wine Wine!," "They call me Speedo but my real name is Mr. Earl," "Jimmy-Mack (when ya comin back?)." We played music for radioactive men.

Mr. Polyester shuffles back inside the lounge, but then they all come back outside, all troop onto the deck. Zeke holds aloft a frothy pitcher of amber ale and Fergus rubs his buzzcut, smiles silently. Drunk Polyester Guy sits back down, waits politely to see what is allowed, if they will allow him any beer.

First she says no: no beer for him.

Ray the bartender's CD player keeps sticking, going *gung gung gung.* The *gung gung* noise gets really irritating after a while. Ray yells, "#35, gorgonzola and jerk chicken!" A minute or two passes *(gung gung gung)* and Canoe Woman relents.

"Give him a shot," she says. She gives the orders. "Give him a shot."

"That would constitute assault," says Zeke, not moving. I don't like people who use the word constitute when they don't need to use the word constitute. Zeke the cool cucumber goes down in my estimation. Zeke stays very still.

"He'll pay me this week," Canoe Woman says. "Give him a shot. He'll pay. Right?"

"Right."

Zeke pours into Drunk Polyester Guy's glass, doesn't stop

pouring, and beer spills all over Drunk Polyester Guy's polyester crotch. Zeke and Canoe Woman laugh at his wet crotch.

"Aw *sonofagun,* Zeke," says Drunk Polyester Guy calmly. He's
being made to eat shit and has decided to take it. Now he has
to walk among the female college students with his pants wet.

Students at tables talk of money to be made tree planting
up in Prince George, a new marketing company in Vic West
with a position open; one blond woman with dark eyebrows
talks of sailing her twenty-six-foot boat among the grey whales
and dolphins all the way from Canada to Mexico. They have
options, suntans, outdoor adventures, and their sky glows like
a watch dial. Drunk Polyester Guy says, *"Sonofagun,* Zeke."

"I demand a certain something, I want a *go-getter,* someone
who'll act without worrying about 'consequences."

"That's me," says Canoe Woman, "to a T. I went to seven
different elementary schools."

"Just good business practices, so yeah ..."

"Industry," adds Fergus.

"Yes, industry"

Drunk Polyester Guy cuts in, "You may not always agree
with what I say but when I say it ..."

She says, "I could make more with *him* in ten minutes.
Some swinger you are. I discovered this place."

"No! I did. I pay a pitcher, pay nachos (fuck this noise), pay
this, pay that . ."

"You buy a tank of gas and talk about it for months." Zeke
says, "When they say *petty* crime, what do they mean?" Drunk
Polyester Guy sputters, "I don't have a black box

thing, like on a 747 (I mean face facts), you know check every minute of my life, check my *contributions* for chrissakes."

"Your many contributions. Throw quarters around like man-hole covers."

"I see now I should've kept detailed records. I see you have a different viewpoint, so yeah . . . I steered you onto a thing or two, we have *history*. That wasn't pin money. Was that chump change, that travel agency job? We have history, had a done deal. (Look at these pants, I wish these damn pants would dry out, I gotta hit the friggin' can like crazy)."

"Yes, our deal. There was a deal. I registered it with the Bureau of Official Deals. I took out extra 'deal' insurance on it, case it fucked up on us (as per usual). I took out fucking spilt-milk insurance. The deal is silk, the deal is clad in iron, and it's also a hedge against inflation and it doubles as money on the motel bed, and it cures dandruff and your fabled impotence."

Zeke is silent as Canoe Woman rambles. I watch but I can't read Zeke.

"I can owe you," says Polyester Man. "I feel my luck changing."

"Sure, okay, you can 'owe' me."

"The deal is dead?"

"The deal is altered slightly now. Things are fluid right this moment, right Zeke?"

"Fluid. I like fluids. It's the hour to be drunken — your health!" toasts Zeke, lifting a glass.

"Well yes you know, health *is* important," allows Canoe Woman. "I believe the key is to sleep at night and hang out with good people. Live by the sea. Eat a balanced diet."

"Yeah, a balanced diet," repeats Zeke.

"So tell me your diet, Zeke," says Drunk Polyester Guy.

"Let's see, the four food groups: sugar, alcohol, caffeine." Zeke's a comedian.

"Ha," says Polyester Man. "I believe that's three."

"Have you? Health? Wealth?" asks Zeke.

"I sure try. I'm pretty okay that way. I try for balance."

With impeccable timing Drunk Polyester Guy bumps the plastic table's edge. They all clutch glasses, keep them upright during this minor earthquake, study the Brussels lace shifting inside the glasses, hold their tense posture longer than they need to, as if waiting for a Tijuana photographer and drinking on a cancelled debit card.

"You the man," mutters Zeke finally, drolly. "Care for a vitamin?"

"What if the vitamin makes my body stop making its own vitamins?"

"Enough about our little health kick," says Canoe Woman.

"Speaking of health," Drunk Polyester Guy says, "I ran over a dog on the way here, mutt just trotted out, stupid dog tongue hanging out, stupid dog looking the wrong way down the avenue, BAM!, weird feeling wiping out Lassie, thought that's not good, that's bullshit, nail a fucking dog, not a good omen."

"Dog dead?"

"Thought it must be dead but the crazy dog rolled a few times, got up, and ran away"

"You follow it?"

"No, my car was blocking traffic. Oh Judas Priest, I can't wait anymore," says Drunk Polyester Guy, his face like different parts of breaking stone. "I'm going to piss myself, I gotta hit the friggin' can."

Young people stare and snicker at his wet pants as he passes, as Drunk Polyester Guy cuts through the white plastic tables and pretty umbrellas open like blue eyes under the pretty blue sky.

The same table the next afternoon has a full pitcher and an empty pitcher. A crushed cigarette package caught at an angle inside the empty pitcher. Beside the pitcher is a jumbo bag of orange nacho chips, a kind and size and bright colour not sold here in the lounge. India Pale Ale under pressure and made from barley malt, yeast, hops, and water; Virginia blend tobacco held in silk paper; Mexican corn chips with a sprinkling of food colouring and BHT (to *preserve freshness!*).

The bountiful earth and globe plays our mysterious, industrious servant, our happy uranium mine. We can't see it but the vein-blue sea hides just down the hill. There always seems to be a man's sodden body hiding in the pretty harbour (*What do you do with the drunken sailor?*). The CD player is functioning, aiming a flawless laser at Pavement's "Slanted & Enchanted." We do a good imitation of rife life here on the pine hill.

Zeke sits behind his prescription sunglasses and walrus mustache and his thin poker face. Canoe Woman wears giant wrap-around sunglasses, those huge black plastic jobbies. Now they both have shades. Drunk Polyester Guy is not with them today, is noticeable by his absence.

Canoe Woman pulls her chair away from the table's blue umbrella, from its shadow She lifts her feet onto another chair. She has short legs and bright white sneakers. Her face to the sun, huge rhomboid sunglasses, chin thrust out, tilting her face to catch some rays.

"Sunsets. People always talking about sunsets as if that's something special. Do I care? Fill a book with what I don't recall about sunsets."

"I was in Hawaii once," Zeke says. "Unbelievable sunset. People applauded."

"Something good," she says. "I gave him something." Secret birds move in the bush around the deck, speaking the local language of a body in the water and dogs rolling on the avenue. Canoe Woman's face looks pleased with itself, light eyes hiding under strip of black plastic, hidden there like a husky's bleach eye. The angle of Canoe Woman's face says she's on a happy thing now, the angle of her face says that Jack and Jill are proceeding up what constitutes a hill with guarded optimism.

"That's just fine," Zeke allows.

A plane passes overhead: John Travolta silently flying over us. He owns a 737, owns a fleet. He flies the world, puts one of his planes on auto-pilot, walks back to the can with a sheepish grin and nice haircut, puts one of his planes down at the airport, rents a pleasing red convertible, and comes for high tea at the Empress Hotel. He likes this railroad hotel on the harbour. He has *juice.* Because he has *juice* they take care of him at the Empress, keep the rabble away at tea, keep us away from his table.

"You've never been to Hawaii." Canoe Woman speaks, staring ahead, not shifting her skull, her Prince Valiant cut, her bleach husky eyes hidden.

A movie star's white plane catches light where it is placed high over muscled men in radioactive tunnels, high over the Chinese graveyard's bachelor bodies and bonehouse facing onto chained logbooms and surging kelp and granite. A tiny white plane climbs over the golden volcano, climbs each black square of the woman's brand new lenses.

Cougar

Motor to the mega mall and the mall moves me to a minor rage. I get in a fight with two women in the mall parking lot, a mother-daughter tag team. Then in the woods a sleek cougar nearly takes my head off, but I said ix-nay.

The story was, I was going to chop us a free Christmas tree, but feeling base and mortal and morbid and pretty fine I collected every damn pill in the trailer, including Flintstones and Aspirin and iron and old tiny Infant Tylenol bottles. What the hell, I'll try anything once. In my pockets I had a dog's breakfast of pills and I felt like a dog, felt lower than a snake's belly.

Things had gone wonky. No jobs in the woods, our old mill sold to foreigners, and foreigners shut it down tight. They don't live here. New softwood agreement too, and Asia gone down the tubes, so we're going right with them, they sneeze and we blow our nose. A letter falls into my black mailbox: they talk of markets, infrastructure, capital costs, mergers, new realities. I imagine them fine-tuning this letter in a meeting over Danish and mineral water. Do they actually know any more than we do?

My tiddly little house is for sale but it's never going to sell because every nice little house is for sale there. I pawned the Husqvarna and moved down island. Everyone laid off. We're global now.

No money for presents. Wet weather: sore elbow, trick knee, bad back, feel I'm hobbling, falling apart, and my K car is acting up since it got rear-ended and the physio making me wear a stu pid collar on my neck. A mild buffet of arthritis and angst in my bones, and my K car is not OK, the Reliant is less than reliant.

I was not, it seemed, lying on a sunny beach, I was not going to Disneyland after creaming the opposition, I was not leaning into a forest of microphones.

It's hard to explain suicidal tendencies. No one detail gets you, but little things add up, little things eat at you. No one uses signal lights and every busker is convinced he can play har-monica. These things kill me.

Drear faces, substantially altered by winter, marked by weak-ness, marked by woe, shadowed, teeth crooked and dun that were straight and white last summer, whole childhoods per-verted, lost, gone down with Asia and you wake up to learn the world is no longer your bright laboratory.

Regarding my mega mall parking lot argument: an old woman and daughter, both smug and slatternly in some japscrap car, stole my parking spot, even as I backed into it. I began to feel I don't recognize this good old world anymore and I am sick of being a *recipient*. Sick of rolling snake-eyes when I want the dice to come up boxcars. Once this world was sweet as the low rumble of sixteen poolballs dropping as one; now I'm a bozo arguing over a stupid parking spot.

That same night I motored past a Christmas tree lot. All those strung lights and exiled, pointy-headed trees leaning around a little trailer used to cheer me up, but instead of good cheer, all I could think of was the tiny newspaper clipping that said the singer of the Tacoma garage band, the Wailers, died in a fire in the trailer on a Christmas tree lot just like this one I drove by. The Wailers were a wild band I really liked way back when, same time as the Sonics, both power pop punks from 1963 or so. I drove by, rain drumming, my car and head like an empty tin of British biscuits. The Wailers had some great tunes on Etiquette Records: "Out of Our Tree," "Hang Up," "You Aren't Using Your Head," "Bad Trip." Maybe they covered "Louie Louie." Have to dig out my old vinyl.

Have to do *something* when Christmas starts to seem like a humungous tax, an annual root canal, to seem alien and overly familiar. To light out, I decided, to the dark woods, into the bush, into a valley to think about things.

Weird weather in the firs on the edge of a continent, wind over the dead ships and lost harbours, stop and go storms jumping off the ocean, wind punching through treetops and stopping abruptly. Strange lulls, torn green branches on the forest floor and crashing sea vibrating rock miles away. Don't like the weather here, they say, just wait ten minutes.

They have said these same words to me every place I've lived or visited.

I tracked through the false infinity of ferns and firs and oak and owls, hiking and humming, *If you go into the woods today, you're in for a big surprise.* I hiked up over rocks, then down a rocky draw, into a bit of a jog moving downhill. Sometimes it's easier to run than hold back.

I was jogging along and WHAM! Like being hit between shoulder blades by speeding bicycle.

Mayday! Mayday! some automatic voice in me thought. *AAOOGA! Bogey at three o'clock.* A small thrilled monster with saliva and bad breath riding my neck and we rolled in a tense frenzy. Noises against me, a cat's mouth and breathing inside its throat, a rush of wind in some pipeline above, bass notes fumbling as we rolled in rocks and moss and sword ferns, and I thought, illogically of course, my face smushed in the rocks and moss, I will kill myself when I'm damn well ready to go and perhaps because of global factors beyond my control, but just this instant some sadass cut-rate panther with a wild face and bad table manners is not going to cut me down out of the blue without so much as a hello sailor.

I didn't know it then, but the cat tore me up a bit, tore my scalp and ear, shoulder, back, but it could have been worse. The cat fell off with my neckbrace collar in its teeth. Maybe the physio's collar helped. The little cougar shook the white collar, then turned back to gaze at me, the real thing, pink meat in pink skin. The cat's fur was out like it was going for a punk look, a trendy looking dude or dudette, ears twitching and rotating like radar, big Oriental face, mouth twisted, white chin, dark where the whiskers poked out and some good looking teeth with drool falling out, which adds greatly to anyone's street cred.

My drool dried up severely.

Luckily my Christmas cougar was a skinny paltry thing, not full grown, and I believe a female, not a big stud tomcat, and not knowing how to really hunt proficiently, or I'd be dead meat and not telling this yarn, I'd be remains with some dirt and leaves raked over me by the cat.

Remains. I suddenly knew, despite my pockets filled with pills, that I did not want to be unidentified human remains, bones scattered around the woods, bits partly buried by animals in a secret funeral, wallet found years later with two-dollar bills in it like that hiker I read about in the mountains.

I was not going to kill myself. My cockeyed world tilted, turned. I wish I could say I became magically happy, but I was not happy. More like muleheaded.

Remains: my neighbour, a university lady, hires me for odd jobs. I have helped her bury pigs. She dresses the pigs in flannel shirts, denim, sunglasses. We buried one pig in a pretty prom dress and white gloves.

I dig the holes for the university lady and she pays me. She studies the dressed pigs after they rot in the shallow graves, sees what insects and beetles are present after one day, three days, a fortnight, year. Police check with the university lady when they need to know how long a body has been in the woods.

The university lady seems to enjoy her work. I don't like to be there when we dig up what I have come to think of as Arnold from the fine old TV show *Green Acres*. I didn't want to become Arnold, even though I thought I came into the woods to become Arnold.

The tan cougar feinted, put its head forward and trotted at me again, skinny but an impressive piece of work, muscles and moving parts leaping at you like you're a big gingersnap it's going to break in two. What my dad called a puma or a panther. In the highway ditches now the government uses expensive panther pee to scare deer away from the road, away from the voters.

Rare to see a cat in the bush, no matter how often you go in, and I've been in the bush a lot. They're good at hiding and are more active after dark. This is rare. This one came out of hiding to try me on for size and I knew I wanted to get out and tell someone about this impressive little creature wielding muscle and razors if I could still get out, get out of the woods before dark drops, dark so early now in December.

The young cat eyed me, ears pinned back, small lower jaw dropped in a snarl, springing at my shoulders. I felt naked even with my folding saw and hardware-store gloves and heavy coat and boots. I ducked and turned but still got knocked over from the cat's force. I think my grandfather's heavy old mackinaw helped deflect her dark claws. How does such a skinny creature generate such amazing force? It was like being boarded by Eric Lindros.

In pure panic I got my old workboots up and kicked the

small cougar, but not before she sliced me on the shins. I had a blurred close-up of curved canines, black gums, and white chin, her noise and cylindrical weight driving in at me and turning back and I went crazy, shrieking like a fishmonger the entire time, using my boots, kicking her several good ones in the pale muscled gut and soft snout, her low centre of gravity and loose skin, her nose bleeding, head down. She tried to get one paw up around me like a drunk, both of us rolling around and scrapping, and then in the hurlyburly this moaning cat shit on me — no kidding, let go like a semi-automatic semi-liquid weapon.

I jumped about three yards trying to get away from that, found a handy hunk of fir and winged it and got her in the face with the wood and she didn't like that. I cut her smooth broad nose, and she paused to peer at this prey that can throw things and was recently sprayed in runny cat scat.

What a world: slide into the woods feeling sensitive and Hamlet-like melancholy, feeling a fine fellow, albeit an anti-social suicide who'd like to blow up the mall, and does Mother Nature smile on you and proffer blackberries and real cream? No, Mother Nature says here is what I think of your finicky brooding.

Maybe at the mega mall I should have shit on them, like the cat did.

You can't *back* into a parking spot, the daughter sneered.

Yeah, you can't back in, they chorused with their arms folded: stealing a spot and then feeling on the side of right. I had pulled forward to allow the parked car to leave and then

I started backing in. They zigzagged in, stealing from me and then blaming me for having a reverse gear! I sputtered in inarticulate rage and wanted dearly to smack their heads together like coconuts but didn't because I was raised right, unlike some others I could mention.

In the bush I had to walk backwards a mile or two and think about things while stepping very carefully in tripwire blackberry canes and salal, bloody hard work uphill and down and stinking of cougar shit. An altered sense of time. I walked backwards trying to look large and swearing at the little puma, though it is hard to sound tough while retreating constantly.

The hungry animal followed me step for step, calmly placing her hind paw exactly where the front paw had stepped, stalking me in expired leaves and trees trying to live in rock and rucked landscape, skinny cat making yowling panther noises. It doesn't jump but stalks me step for step, following me like a machine, eyes in fearsome concentration, both of us thinking, and I waved a folding saw and waved a worthless stick like a B-movie pirate, a branch of punky oak that was about to fall to pieces, but the cat didn't know that. I walked backwards, waved a stick, and went back in time.

Decades back my dad told me of a big tom that weighed as much as he did, a big cat that would lope along beside fleeing livestock and calmly flatten any goat or calf or sheep it wanted; one blow and it's down dead. A big tom can leap twenty or thirty feet from a perch and it can snap your neck.

I knew that a woman died defending her kids from a cougar in the Interior, and a few years back a cat killed a child up the coast. When I was driving north from California to B.C. some years back, a woman in Northern California, a famous Olympic runner, was training in the woods, running fast and was jumped from behind and killed, and I was driving through the red-woods and heard about it and was 'amazed, but didn't know it would be visited on me later.

I knew this cat could kill me and that impressed me, made things clear, and I knew the mall scene with the twin harpies was not important, even though I wanted to bend their windshield wipers into pretzels. It clears your mind wonderfully to walk backwards in the backwoods and wonder will you die from four sabre teeth or five claws attached to paws the size of country pancakes.

I walked backwards, went into my past, and recalled all the old jobs I'd had: truckdriver, digging wells, digging clams by lantern light, spark-watching, whistle punk, faller for a dollar, bucker for a buck, busboy in Duncan, dryland sort and chainsaw maestro, choker, joker, smoker, timber cruiser, a snoozer, a scaler, feeding the green chain, working in a box factory, riding the milk train, and riding an orange forklift with a big battery on the back. Smoke meant money but now all the jobs are gone up in smoke, love's labour lost. I walked backwards and thought of burying pigs in the woods. It's legal but still there is something illicit about the act of burying a body in the woods.

I thought of the singer for the Wailers dying in the burning trailer and the space heater that killed him. Did his Christmas trees catch fire too?

I have too many friends dead of mundane things. Widow-maker branches blown down on their head or a chainsaw into an artery, or touching the wrong wire, or porch-climber wine in your hand, or just some greasy creations you eat once too often.

They jack-knifed their logging truck, or they drove a 4 x 4 backwards off a cliff in the snow, thinking they're just turning around, two guys and two women. The whole truck drops backwards with them in it, hood aimed up, when the driver was just trying to turn it around, trying to get them back home. Imagine their surprise, the terrible dashboard light on their faces.

I walked backwards cursing at the cougar and remembering all the battered buses and muddy trucks, the company crummies with your black lunchbox and sugary coffee and long muddy drives into the trees, driving logging roads to the show and driving out the same way, hours and hours, the tiny taverns by the bay much later at last light, trees by the parking lot, water a silver curve at the picture windows, wind rushing the glass, and drinking feels good and logical. It's dark and you should be heading home, *true,* but not right away. There are pickled eggs and perfect clubhouse sandwiches and one more round, oyster shells piled outside, beer cases and kegs piled inside, enough draft to float a coalship, float a peeler, start a fight in the parking lot, the crews and friends and enemies and gilt-edged girlfriends and ex-girlfriends who never thought you were like this, what does anyone really know of anyone, and your friends die too young, play harmonica well, and drive innocently just one foot too far over the cliff in the snow, the jilted joking faces and farces, the smiling hours I thought were disposable, the smiling hours I thought would never run out.

One young woman from the 4 x 4 crawled out at the base of the giant cliff, crawled for miles looking for me to help her and I'd had a few, I saw her crawling like a turtle in the head-lights and stopped, thinking, What in Christly tarnation are these crazy schoolkids up to now? and then we found out what had happened and the Whole town in shock.

I was driving my '68 Cougar; that was a very nice car but I had to sell it some time ago to a child who I knew would crash it on Kangaroo Road, wreck my good '68 Cougar. I saw him drive away and envisioned his head busting right through the windshield and my nice green car wrapped around a tree up by the reservoir.

How you miss that job you cursed and the guys that ragged on you; you miss the car that broke down, the life that never was, but seems sweet now in retrospect.

The cougar's face is a mask. When kittens their eyes are blue but later they turn yellow. Her dark eyes are almost crossed — strange, hypnotic eyes, circles in a triangle, her eyes round and slitted and triangular at the same time, a weird geometry, her dark eyes fierce and relaxed, like a good fighter, a boxer's broad nose, fur scrunched up on her nose like a tiny rug piled up.

It stared at me and scrunched its nose, mouth pulled back, four good curving teeth, two up, two down, a perfect clamp.

Teeth bared, that cougar walked me back over muck and rock and hill and dale to adrenalin and feeling; that cougar walked me back to sensation, blood, good bread, IPA, choice, the pull of home, to draw breath. I moved my brain in the woods.

Out of the pitch and pine and turpentine the puma walked me back to life. The cat quit following me when it saw the rusty K car and it melted away in two seconds, gone like a ghost, no regret on its face. Perhaps a slight wince, didn't approve of the dull car.

Clothes cut up, and lacerations starting to hurt more, after the fact, like in hockey, when you don't notice some welts until later. Covered in blood, stinking and shaking after I stopped and sat and thought about my date, my escort, how close I'd been.

Stupid car starts. In reasonably reliant Reliant I drove into town, past a Christmas tree lot, and I thought again of the burnt guy from the Wailers, but it was all right: I'll have some grog or eggnog in memory of him and his old fuzztone band. I believe he'd appreciate that more than any moping or mooning about death and gases and fire.

Stars and constellations floating like shirts in the December sky, Saturn's rings and Jupiter's moons moving right over her white shining trailer. Her porch and door lit yellow; tiny blue and red lights glowing on two shrubs. I limped through the silky colours, saw her reading on the couch.

Her kitchen was warm and toasty; soup smelling good on the stove, her whole trailer creaking when you walk. It creaks like a ship, creaks like me. The soup sits on a flame, and flames killed the singer for the Wailers, but soup will heat up my guts, restore me. Soup equals life at this moment. Poor cat starving; it didn't eat me. I hope it has an okay Christmas, finds a few fat rabbits or a little blacktail or a chihuahua, wrapped in a sweater like a burrito.

Did you get a tree?

Uh. Not quite. Guess I forgot the tree.

How can you forget? Were you out drinking again? What happened to your pants? You look ... is that blood? You get in a fight or run into some wild woman?

Well yeah. I did just that. Both. A real hellcat she was.

I thought of the cougar's face. It thought it had me dead to rights but there was also a kind of glum resignation and hooded resentment there in its face. A lost nation. Both of us missed a connection, lost a world. I tried to tell her this in the kitchen.

She knew something was up. She knew I was telling her something and she went quiet because she's smart and she waits for me to cut the crap.

I have no real job and no irons in the fire and no cash on the barrelhead and there are no mills hiring and no king salmon run past our window. No one in Bedford Falls brings me baskets of money and the only job I can wangle is burying pigs for the university lady, but I am back in the world and I am going to have some good steaming chowder and after that a good beer, and maybe a crossword puzzle in ink, as I am careful and reckless. And maybe some screaming Buffalo wings — suicide wings we used to call them — and maybe clams in a metal bucket and another beer and maybe a bath with some salt for my multiple slashes from the cat, and her big soft bed with the creaking filigree headboard rattling Morse code to the wall.

I was out of the woods. I was not remains, not eating hospital food. In terms of rolling dice, I now felt I was throwing boxcars.

Have yourself a very merry Christmas, spoke a red bakelite radio on the oilcloth. Decided I liked that radio.

Damn right, Merry Christmas to you, I said back. That soup ready? It smells great.

Please, she said, testing the waters.

I said the magic word and was rewarded, and I thought, My house up island ever sells I'll look for a '67 or '68 Cougar, a sharp looking car, light green paintjob, pretty glittery paint, and I'll put good tires on it, get a grip, *control.*

I see myself perched behind a clean dark windshield, my brain steering the car, and every red and green wire in my world working. Reflected in my shining chrome are bright planets and dark woods flashing past us like the briefest of seasons.

Streetcleaner

An elephantine streetcleaning machine roars our tiny street, water gushing gutters, big brown brushes spinning foam and sand. The machine's driver swerves niftily around two blue cars parked in front of our house. My mother peers out the kitchen window, romps excitedly down the stairs to our basement. *Wake up! The streetcleaner is doing our street! Move your cars!* I was working 'as a janitor on a graveyard shift. All I recall from this part of my life is sleeping and being woken, coming inside and going outside, sleeping and being woken again. In that basement in the groggy ground I slept and wondered, would a future ever come rumbling up the street under that perfect tunnel of elms, and would I look back nostalgically to that time when there was no future?

Groaning, muttering, my sister and I pull on last night's clothes, find car keys, start balky engines, but all the time careful to preserve delicate cobwebs of stupor. We coax our blue cars across the street and crawl once more into warm sheets. Zzzzz.

The streetcleaner rumbles back the opposite direction, spots the same two blue cars in his way again. What the hell? the driver wonders.

The giant machine curves around them once more. Two dark brown trails on the road etch the shape of a bass fiddle, the shape of a woman's hips. Would those new spy satellites, he wonders, notice his perfect design?

My mother wakes my sister and me again. *No! Move your cars! The streetcleaner! He can't do our street!*

We start up the cars again, drive the cars to the next street by the ravine, and step back into the tiny kitchen. This time we stay up, put on Mr. Coffee, peruse the papers.

The driver pulls the huge streetcleaning machine over at the park up the road. The driver climbs down, stretches on grass under elms and magpies.

My mother runs up the street to where the driver lies on dead winter grass with his red plaid thermos and plastic lid full of chicken noodle soup.

The cars are out of the way now! she explains happily. *You can clean our street now!*

When I was young my mother hummed Irish airs. She was alive in Dublin before anyone had a radio. People sang rebel songs, put their hands to concertinas and hurdy-gurdies, had religion, had dead siblings planted in Glasnevin graveyard.

I fall out of the womb, listen to Jimi Hendrix. What do I

care about the old rebel songs? Irish airs: she never names the Irish airs.

And my mother never speaks of what the gruff street-cleaning man told her to do. In a silent way she wanders back to us.

I was a janitor, knowing what it is to clean up after other people — a kind of glum rage touching every act, rage an engine moving you through two worlds until you fall on the mattress and try to disappear under the pier.

Coffee break done, the raucous machine fires up, slouches bluntly, hugely toward the next street in the giant circuit board, where my sister and I have installed our blue cars. We repeat this roaring minuet across the manifest city grid.

Subterranean Homesick Blues

Our house hides in tall trees and my fake rolltop perches at a high window. I admire arbutus and oak, fir and fern, gaze into dappled boreal light. Red freighters and whitewater islands cut up the blue strait, and I am smug, as if I arranged it all.

My desk floats high in an airy adult world, but my thoughts drift, my mind travels down the stairs, past my kids playing in their basement, out the ugly carport, over the Rocky Mountains and childhood prairies, to my parents' bungalow, to the stairs I used to leap down, thunder down, into the primal basement.

In my childhood home in Edmonton my parents set up a sensible form of apartheid: adults huddled upstairs, futilely trying to isolate themselves from their raucous rabble offspring down in the bunker.

The kitchen was Checkpoint Charlie and we were gyrating down in the basement, a savage underground nation, wrestling, shouting, rabbit-punching, poring over bra ads, listening to

CKUA or spinning my older brothers' records on an old combo TV-console stereo. I grew up on a weird mix of psychedelia, blues, bubble gum pop: the Ventures, Big Brother & the Holding Co., Iron Butterfly, the Collectors, Buffalo Springfield, Dusty Springfield, Herman's Hermits, John Mayall's Blues-breakers, the Monkees, and the Mothers of Invention LP, *Freak Out.*

My Junior Scientist chemistry set exploded down there: my parents' white ceiling tiles splattered a gorgeous cobalt blue while Dylan sang *Johnny's in the basement, mixing up the medicine.* In the basement we played frantic table-hockey, crashed our racetrack cars, burnt up the old train set.

Down in the basement my younger brother laid elaborate Rube Goldberg traps for me. Once Martin simply placed a bucket of water atop a slightly open door, but he forgot and walked under his own trap and soaked himself.

Another trap was more ingenious: he ran a long piece of string from the doorknob to a turntable tonearm with an Englebert Humperdink record spinning and the volume cranked to Spinal Tap eleven. I snuck in late, trying to be quiet. I opened my bedroom door and the needle jerked onto the spinning vinyl and I jumped in my skin as Englebert bellowed "Please Release Me" loud enough to shake our parents from their bed.

I had my revenge. One night our parents were out of town and I heard Martin negotiate the kitchen door and veer immediately to his room. I could interpret these signs. He was avoiding humans because of a precarious mental state brought on by privately funded research into how many cans of beer he and his gang could carry in their golfbags at the course by the river. My mother had slippers she wore at night, tiny slippers that made a nervewracking *scritch scritch* sound as she inexorably crossed the wide basement floor enroute to grill you about your evening, your sins, see if any signs fit the list she saw in *Reader's Digest,* the *scritch scritch* getting closer and closer, repeated like the clock in *High Noon.*

I squished my toes into the dreaded slippers and moved my feet across the basement floor. It sounded exactly like my mother. As I slowly shuffled closer *(scritch scritch)* I could sense tension rising in my younger brother's room: *What's she doing here? I'm trapped. I thought they were at the lake!*

I was pleased with the psychological aspects of this slow torture, and even Martin showed some admiration, but my success meant I would have to watch my back for a few years because our family, like the Godfather, thought revenge a dish best tasted cold. We would wait each other out. The original slight might be forgotten, but our devotion to getting even was timeless, the one true faith.

Martin and my younger sister Clare had an odd game where they flung billiard balls across the pool table at each other's fingers , had to hold their fingers in place as long as possible to prove they weren't chicken. This seemed skill-testing and worthwhile until the eight ball flew off the table and cracked the toilet.

Anything endangering plumbing was *verboten,* an indictable offence to the Old Testament gods above us in adult-land. We began working over our alibis like jailhouse lawyers. Deflecting blame and assigning guilt occupied much of my child-hood time, was our equivalent of paperwork.

Martin and I had a questionable form of entertainment for those long dark winter nights: we'd fish out reject shirts from the closet, shirts that had travelled light years out of style. We'd put on a shirt, stand like sartorial gladiators, and attack, tear-ing each other's shirt into shreds. We'd stop, calmly button up another shirt, and flail at each other again, shirt by stupid shirt, until there was little left but rags on the floor and red welts carv-ing our neck and arms while people went shirtless in China.

Occasionally my sainted mother would tire of the racket and fights and stupidity and throw the brawling bunch of us outside into a snowbank. Then she would lock the door. Can you blame her?

In my ridiculous high school days, I saw a good local band at the Corona Hotel on Jasper Avenue. Friends and I drank a table full of warm flat draught, what served as an excuse for beer in those dark days before microbrews, drank and ate about eighty-five packs of beer-nuts, a minor addiction. We were un-derage, but the legal age had just gone down from twenty-one to eighteen and there was some confusion about what an eigh-teen-year-old looked like. Also, I had giant sideburns, smoke-stacks, that made me look older. Sometimes we rode the trolley using green children's tickets, then piled off and walked coolly, nervously, into the Klondiker Tavern.

In the Corona bar several friends stood to go to the wash-room, but I climbed the stairs to the exit, thinking we were leaving. Outside I was alone and confused. Where did everyone go?

I thumbed home to the parents' bungalow, back to the basement. I wanted to pass out, but suspected I might soon be sick, talking on the great white phone, buying a Buick, a technicolor yawn. I had that old time feeling.

Sleepy, wearing only Woodward's $1.49 Day underwear, I lay on the bathroom floor beside the toilet, waiting for this dispatch from the interior of the continent, making myself comfortable with a roll of toilet paper under my head as a pillow.

I awoke from a refreshing nap covered chin to loins in a mysterious unpleasant substance, and my spitfire mother was forcing the bathroom door, saying accusingly, "That's not beer, my brothers in Dublin drank beer, that must be heroin!"

I remember finding her comment exceedingly funny, which must have infuriated her. I laughed and, still lying on the floor clad only in underwear and undigested lager and beer-nuts (hardly a dignified podium), tried to convince her that Martin must have thrown up all over my inert form whilst I innocently napped alongside the commode. This seemed to me a plausible explanation. We tried to blame Martin whenever an opportunity arose, the way we piled our vegetables on his plate when he wasn't looking.

I rose from my loutish repose, freshened up, and fell into bed ready to dream of naked redhaired mermaids wearing seaweed and red sunglasses while my puzzled mother arranged pots and buckets around her disappointing son.

One bedroom we nicknamed the Submarine Room because it was long, narrow, and lacked oxygen and light. You could sleep forever in the Submarine Room, outside of Mountain Standard Time.

My mother claimed she never slept a wink and she was greatly suspicious of anyone else getting any sleep and so spent much of her sainted life shaking our shoulders and dragging us from the submarine beds, calling out, Get up you lazy louts! Get a job you dirty ould stop-outs!, even though we already had jobs. Need be she'd throw buckets of icewater or start the lawnmower on the rug between our beds.

If the cleaning lady was coming we got even less sleep because we had to clean up for the cleaning lady and then were cast out like orphans to wander icy streets with bleary eyes and pounding heads, to wander like freezing zombies to 124th Street and a grumbling greasy breakfast in Betty's Lunch.

Clean up for the cleaning lady! Those words still fill me with dread.

Prim, primitive romances flourished in the basement. My good friends Bill and Paula were going out briefly, but every time Bill went to the bathroom Paula and I would neck madly on the couch, then act "normal" when Bill came back out. These liplocking sessions were amazingly fun and erotic and a tonic for the blood, and I think Bill knew and got a kick out of our being together; he was amazingly tolerant and wanted his friends to be happy.

For some it transpires in a penthouse, a rolling yacht, a narrow car-seat, a wide-body 747. My delayed deflowering arrived in a basement (I'm not telling whose). I had tried and tried, toiled and moiled, rolled and tumbled, but I became convinced the actual act was too complicated for me and confessed this failing to a new girlfriend. After all my clumsy humiliating experiences, I had, like with high school math, given up. Coitus and logarithms were equally mysterious and unassailable concepts to me.

This fine young woman felt sorry for me, and she comforted me with hugs and kisses. One thing led to another. Nanoseconds later, after consummation had proved to be rather simple, she said, "There's nothing wrong with you," a note of suspicion in her voice, as if I had pulled a fast one (it *was* a quick one, but I had not pulled a fast one).

I was so very *grateful* for her phrase, her backhanded compliment: *nothing wrong with you.* She let me into a warm intimate world, and I was not doomed to some sexual Nebraska, some solitary freezing bachelor basement.

I broke so many basement windows. Once I whacked a golf ball toward the ravine but hit a low retaining wall. The ball rocketed back toward my head. I ducked and the ball kept moving through space and time and fractured a large picture window. It was not the last window.

When I was almost thirty and back yet again in the parents' basement, my life going nowhere, I was downstairs taking shots at the fireplace with a tennis ball and a hockey stick. I was drilling them in and wondering how the Oilers missed me. Then the ball went a little high, hitting up on the brick chimney and the howitzer came tearing back toward my puzzled head. Once more I ducked and the innocent window behind fell to fragments worthy of Cromwell.

Dad trod across the living room, peered down the stairs at me, wondering if he was hallucinating, then turned away without a word, which was worse than a lecture. His son almost thirty and home breaking windows. What a loser! Such travails were supposed to be behind him now in these, his golden years.

Finally I made that last trip up the stairs, travelled past Checkpoint Charlie and into jobs, journeys, other cities, other continents, into matrimony and maternity wards, into used furniture stores looking for tables and highchairs.

My parents sold our childhood house, moved into a high-rise, but now I have my own mortgaged basement, my own raucous kids, my own peel & stick tiles, and I find myself forced into the role of upstairs adult, now I am bellowing at my blond boys, DOWNSTAIRS!! GO DOWNSTAIRS!!

Now my desk is upstairs, in the adult section, and my three beloved boys are busy downstairs flooding my basement. They come in to wash their hands, plug the sink, turn on the water, clean their hands quickly, then gallop from the room shrieking, Last one out's a rotten egg!

Sink plugged, tap running, several inches of water on the carpet, and a freshet flowing to the back door.

Just like *Titanic,* my oldest boy explained happily to his teacher later.

We laughed later but Oh my RAGE at the time. I thought about the rich pleasure I would receive if I held all three blond heads underwater in the brimming steel sink, but I also recalled what my brothers and sisters and I had done to my parents, done to our basement walls and floors. As kids we hooted when my father fought his own floods, laughed at him perched on a plastic bucket over a spewing drain in the floor of the laundry room, Kafka's Bucket-Rider, a Canadian Cuchulainn battling the tide, and we laughed.

I am being punished for that laughter now, paid back with interest.

Robert Fulghum, that coy snake-oil salesman, claims he learnt all he needed in kindergarten. Cute Barney-type idea but for me it was all happening in the basement recesses: we searched in vain for matching socks, hid a stash, snuck puzzlingly devoted girlfriends in the tiny window. The basement held our scratched blues records and homework desks and bookshelves with Lenny Bruce and Sartre and Kerouac and Biggles.

The basement formed the cluttered thought control centre of my childhood and adolescent universe, my addled alma mater, but I don't care to go back for a reunion. False nostalgia about childhood is pointless, false nostalgia gets you sent to the Submarine Room to sleep forever or until my mother comes in scritchy slippers to yank you out of bed by your big toe: *Get up and get a job you dirty ould stop-out!*

No, I like being an adult up here in the trees with the bigger windows watching the sea's blue and white vistas. I like being on top.

Brighten the Corners

In the speeding car's backseat my three boys play an intellectual game where they smash into each other like atoms while I negotiate particularly thrilling corners on Smuggler's Cove Road. To aid their education I honk the horn ("Shave and a Haircut" or "Smoke on the Water"), turn more sharply than needed, or zigzag when no police cars are visible. With relatively low overhead I provide valuable memories and life lessons.

Gabby, three years old and squished in a gruelling series of S-turns, exclaims in a sing-song voice: "I'M GETTING AN-NOY-ING!!" He means I'm getting annoyED but I like his version, as it hints at both words and I can identify with his sentiment. I just spent three weeks alone roaming odd corners of Dublin and London; I'm finding it a challenge to come back to Canada and find I still have kids, to find I still have three kids, and to find I have them all day in some kind of penance for going away and having big fun.

I'm grumpy, my mind's not right, and my face feels made of string. With its double-edged intimations, "I'M GETTING ANNOYING!" seems apropos to me, my loving family, and my speed of light transition to full-time childcare.

ITEM (I've always wanted to write a piece with *ITEM* in it): Working at my desk at midnight, Pavement's "Brighten the Corners" low on the stereo, I also hear the unmistakable sound of my cat throwing up in our basement. New brand of catfood being rejected by the marketplace. I clean huge rainbow-hued heaps from the K-Mart Persian rug, hide the food bowl, and go to bed.

I drop off to sleep, then wake to the rattle and hum of Gabby's talentless struggle with his door knob. I meet with him in the dim groggy hall. Scared by a bad dream, he drags his blanket à la Linus. Perhaps he dreamed he was an adult.

"I want to cuddle," he breathes in a library whisper.

"Cuddle with who?" I whisper back, because his destination seems beyond our bedroom, somewhere toward Mecca.

"With *Sharon,*" he says, a three-year-old not tolerating fools gladly at this hour.

Sharon has to get up early, Sharon needs her sleep. I don't want to wake her, so I play God and coax Gabby back to bed with a Digestive fragment and a sip of water and let him leave the light on, let him brighten the corners. In a few minutes I look in and he's asleep in his new London bobby helmet, I switch the light off.

Moments later it's morning and I'm wiping Gabby's posterior with three steaming face cloths. End the balmy day with cat puke and greet the summer dawn with someone else's fecal matter. Go to grad school to accomplish this. Do not pass Go, do not collect $200. I put on the kettle for tea, open the fridge door. The butter compartment door, spring exhausted, falls open in exquisite timing and hits the cream which flips neatly into the air and drops as if on a bungee cord, but it's not on a bungee cord. Spilt cream in every crevasse and drawer of the fridge. Pull out all the fridge parts and sponge them clean.

Try to carry three cups and fail, spilling orange juice on me and the floor. I'm getting AN-NOY-ING. Explain to the boys why I alone am allowed to employ the F word. Tell them I would be happy to be sent to my room. Clean the fucking floor.

Fatalistic about the world and God now, I check under the guest bed where my cat fled at midnight while I cleaned the first mountains of vomit. There hides one more geological formation, luckily on a flattened cardboard box I had stored there. The cat feigns amnesia.

I tear off the affected square of cardboard and recycle the rest. I chase the boys with a multihued square of cat puke. They scream, thrilled. We're getting in touch with our darker feelings. What daycare could supply this mix of stimulation and fine motor skills? *Father knows best.* Dear dirty Dublin's National Library and church spires, Celtic crosses, oaken pubs, and miles of slummy Joycean backlanes start to seem hallucinatory, an unreal city.

I dress the boys in the same clothes they wore yesterday and give them variations on yogurt and toast and grapes since none of them want exactly what the other has. I could thrash them and serve gruel but I desist.

Wisps of ocean fog blow past the house and big fir and arbutus, reminding me I'm closer to autumn, work, death, Esso payments. I'll build a fire in the afternoon, be of good cheer, wait until the sun crosses a yardarm somewhere on this grumpy planet, and dwell on perfect pints of Smithwick's Ale with a Guinness head in O'Neil's of Pearse Street or the Funnel Bar on Dublin's abandoned City Quay where a fiddle player practises "Come On Eileen" over and over in a room up the steep stairs. Martin, seven, tells Kelly, five, that he heard aliens landing during the night, that aliens like to visit while we sleep.

Martin sells Kelly a black plastic bat (nocturnal not baseball) from the Royal Museum one dollar for the bat and one dollar for showing him how to balance the bat on your nose. This seems a good deal for both. I don't know if aliens or bats influence the next topic (like me, the boys are not big on logic or clear transitions).

Kelly says, "Guess who I hate."

I don't pay much attention. Hate is a cheap commodity compared to earlier moments in my life. Once "I hate you" really meant something, was a memorable scene with a quivering murderous girlfriend. I've been robbed of such panic and pinnacles of emotion. Now it's like saying today is a weekday, now it's like saying Janis Joplin liked a drink or two.

"I'm pointing at who I hate," Kelly says. I expect his tiny finger to compass toward me or one of his brothers but Kelly points up at the light fixture. He hates Rick the Zen electrician?

"Who controls the world?" Kelly asks. Ronald McDonald, I think automatically.

"Who made everything?" China, I decide.

"You hate God?" Martin interjects.

Kelly nods sagely that Martin is correct. I have to laugh even though I should probably be more serious with this topic. My devout parents would have been shocked. I remember as a teen hoping to get close enough to Jesus for just one good punch.

"Why do you hate God?" I ask, curious.

"Because he made *bad things* in the world. That's why," he says lightly, popping a grape into his mouth. "Let's go race bikes in the carport!" he suggests.

"Yeah!" the others say.

End of theological discussion for them, though the sentiments keep echoing in my skull, and mysteriously enough, serve to lift my spirits, dismantle my grumpy mood.

Outside, the boys climb happily on their trikes and plastic tractors . From a window above I watch them; I watch, trying to jettison Europe and its frenetic baggage, its firebombed Irish trains and smoking pubs and the cool canal where my mother's father drowned at the same age I am now. I'm easing into my own verdant canal, easing back into a decent domestic universe, getting less an-noy-ing.

There is a crow with a stern medieval face making eye contact with me; a metal mask staring. Cool Hand Luke, I think: *Got my mind right, boss.*

My boys are too big for trikes and tractors but they postpone graduation from this minor Eden, this childhood mecca, because over the years they have worked out ritualistic orbits and private contests starting at the rainspout in the carport and ending by the Douglas fir down near the driveway's end, a border of their universe where they screech to a halt to pick blackberries after a hardfought race.

Laurel leaves the colour of limes shine in lines of sunlight and red butterflies meander flight-paths high in the fir boughs, in the bright corners of their world.

My three boys smear their mouths and clothes with sour berries, then it's once more into the breech, back into their ordained orbits, hunched like giants over their tiny vehicles and pedalling furiously.

Acknowledgements

Earlier versions of most of these stories have appeared in the following magazines, journals, and anthologies: *Georgia Review, Malahat Review, Prism International, Geist, Washington Square* (NYU), *Northern Lights* (Montana), *Queen's Quarterly, sub-TERRAIN, Zygote, The Reader* (Saint John *Telegraph-Journal), The Wild Life* (Banff), *Monday Magazine, Grain, Front & Centre, Under the Sun* (Tennessee), *American Literary Review, Event, Western Living, The New Quarterly, Best Canadian Stories* 1998 and 1999, *Canadian Fiction Magazine (Pop Goes the Story* anthology), and *Turn of the Story: Canadian Short Fiction on the Eve of the Millennium* (Anansi).

"Burn Man on a Texas Porch was shortlisted for the 1999 O. Henry Prize. "Song from Under the Floorboards" won the Playwrights' Union of Canada 1997-1998 International Monologue Competition.